T

By

Riano D. McFarland

Vanity Inc.

Copyright © 2020 by Riano D. McFarland.

All rights reserved. No part of this book may be reproduced or transmitted in any form or by any means, electronic or mechanical, including photocopying, recording, or by an information storage and retrieval system, without permission in writing from the copyright owner.

This is a work of fiction. names, characters, places, and incidents either are the product of the author's imagination or are used fictitiously, and any resemblance to any actual person, living or dead, events, or locales is entirely coincidental.

Any figures depicted in stock imagery are models, and such images are being used for illustrative purposes only.

This book is dedicated to all of the first responders who stood in the gap, saving lives while the rest of the world took shelter from the storm. One day, the battle against the coronavirus will be won, but the heroic acts of our medical professionals, emergency services personnel, truckers, postal and delivery professionals, and those working to keep our food supply lines open, will never be forgotten.

On behalf of the entire world, we thank you!

THE JOURNAL

CHAPTER 1

It was an old, dusty house.

It was far too large and filled with so many random, mismatched, and disassociated objects that the otherwise sprawling floorplan left Patrice barely enough room to navigate the narrow corridors through the remaining open spaces.

She'd arrived a day earlier, tugging a small U-Haul trailer behind her luxury SUV. Immediately upon entering the house, she realized that her plan to quickly assess the general value of the items and appliances inside, had been a foolhardy one.

Even the musky draft that rushed past her as she opened the front door, seemed to carry the scent of ancient desperation, anxious to escape the confines of a house filled to capacity. Although the current had not yet been restored by the power company, the atmosphere inside the house seemed exceptionally frigid despite the fact that the temperature outside was approaching 100 degrees.

After nearly a full day of wandering the catacombs of the ground floor, snapping photos with her smartphone and using internet reverse image searches, she seemed no closer to determining the origins of most of the objects in the room, than she had been when she began. Aside from the basic living room furniture, most of the items seemed to have been created for specific purposes—none which Patrice as of yet, had been able to identify.

The technician from the power company arrived shortly before nightfall, restoring the electricity, and flooding the building with light which seemed to be, at its best, insufficient. Nevertheless, it did allow Patrice to keep working deep into the night until hunger and fatigue forced her to take a break. After clearing a spot on the cluttered coffee table for the Chinese takeout she'd ordered and her bottled water, she plopped down onto the dusty couch leaning back to visually assess her progress.

The colored sticky note system she used to categorize her findings seemed to have exacerbated the sense of disorder in the room. Now, in addition to the plethora of undefinable objects, there were hundreds of multi-colored sticky notes attached to everything. The green tags indicating items known or positively identified, were vastly outnumbered by the yellow and pink tags attached to items of unclear or unidentified origin, respectively. Looking upward, she realized there were two additional stories above her that appeared to be just as cluttered as the ground floor, which she hadn't even come close to completing yet.

As she sat there nibbling an eggroll and trying to calculate the amount of time, she'd need to finish cataloging the near overwhelming number of unusual items inside the house, a shadow darted across the ceiling at which she'd been blankly staring. Suddenly, her thoughts zoomed back to reality, wondering what might have wandered in through the front door she'd left open the entire day in an attempt to raise the Alaskan tundra-like temperature inside the house.

She sat quietly for a moment, staring motionlessly at the ceiling while waiting to see if the shadow would appear again. She didn't have to wait for long as a silhouette reappeared, apparently crossing the landing near the stairs on the third floor. Halfway across the ceiling, the shadow paused before slowly moving toward the stair rail.

Patrice was instantly gripped by fear! She quietly slipped from the couch onto the floor before quickly crawling around behind it. From there, she could still see the shadow being projected onto the ceiling; however, she was effectively shielded from seeing, or being seen from the actual landing above her. She watched wide-eyed as the shadow seemed to curiously peer over the rail to inspect the floors below before cautiously backing away from it again. Her mind was racing, and her heart was pounding in her chest. Surely, she would have noticed someone walking into the house, even while engrossed in creating her image inventory. The creaky wooden stairs were certainly not ideal for sneaking up and down them, and the maze of shelves and objects winding inside from the front door would have made it impossible for anyone to pass by her undetected. Notably, the layers of cobwebs and dust bunnies adorning the pathway to the antique wooden staircase were abundant and undisturbed and had obviously been that way for quite some time.

After objectively weighing the mental evidence, it occurred to her that the silhouette, while unexpected, was certainly not daunting. In fact, it barely seemed tall enough to peer over the stair rail and hadn't done anything Patrice could definitively perceive as a threat. Suddenly, she felt silly for opting to hide behind the couch when she should probably have simply introduced herself, like a normal sane human being. At a minimum, the food on the coffee table would have been a dead giveaway that someone had recently been seated there.

Hesitantly, she stood up from behind the couch, calling out "Hello. Is anybody here?"

The faint rustling sound coming from upstairs was reminiscent of the panicked scurrying of a small animal discovered near an enticing trash bin. Whatever it was, was obviously trying to avoid being detected and seemed to be retreating into a hiding place. Patrice cautiously approached and climbed the stairs to the second floor, while thinking to herself "*I should have brought the poker from the fireplace. Isn't that what every soon-to-be murder victim does in situations like this?*" For a moment, she actually considered going back for it upon reaching the second-floor landing. She could clearly see the poker in the stand beside the hearth along with the other fireplace accessories.

Cautioning herself not to succumb to baseless fear again, she pivoted to climb the remaining stairs leading up to the third floor;

however, in her right hand she was suddenly gripping the fireplace poker. Her eyes darted quickly back over her shoulder, and she noticed there was now one item conspicuously missing from the accessory stand near the hearth.

Proceeding cautiously, she shouted "Is anyone up there?" There was no response.

The house had stood empty on the large gated estate for nearly four years, and it was entirely conceivable that a squatter had found his way inside, feeling fortunate to have gone undetected for so long. Still, the power had been restored hours ago and it seemed as if every light switch in the house had been flipped to the ON position prior to the service being terminated. It would have been impossible for anyone inside the house to ignore the sudden reappearance of the lights and electricity with the place lit up like Fort Knox.

When Patrice reached the third-floor landing, every door on that level was open except for the one at the far end of the hallway opposite the stairs. Cautiously approaching it, she placed her ear against the door before softly knocking and saying "Hello? Is anyone in there? I'm the new owner of the house."

From the other side of the door, she heard a timid voice quietly saying "Miss Patrice? Is that you?"

"Yes," replied Patrice. "Patrice LaFleur, and what is your name?"

It had been almost twenty years since Patrice last visited her aunt Naomi inside the house, and anyone she'd known back then had either moved or passed away long ago. In fact, when she heard the soft footfalls of someone approaching the door from the other side, it occurred to her that the only person who'd ever called her Miss Patrice was the imaginary friend she invented for the elaborate tea parties she'd written about inside the pages of her secret journal. Furrowing her brow, she squinted while attempting to remember the little girl's name, and as the door slowly began to open, it came to her. The girl's name was...

"Nadine," said the familiar girl standing in the doorway. "My name is Nadine. Don't you remember me?"

Patrice just stood there. While a trillion brain cells fired simultaneously, searching for the right words to express the phenomenon occurring directly in front of her, the only thing that left her lips was silence.

Standing across from her, Patrice remembered the solitude of being summarily dropped off and abandoned by her mother, who's addiction to prescription drugs had overridden any maternal instincts that might have survived her string of near-fatal recreational drug overdoses. When they pulled up to the house, she'd followed her mother up the porch steps wearing her bright yellow raincoat and boots and carrying one small suitcase of her belongings. Her mother told her to wait there while she brought up the rest of her things. Instead, she jumped into the driver's seat and sped away, leaving Patrice alone on the porch as her taillights disappeared into the darkness, blurred by sheets of torrential rain.

It was the last time she ever saw her mother, and while the confusion and outrage were clearly imprinted onto her aunt's face, Naomi ushered Patrice into her home and up the long, rounded staircase. She could now clearly recall the seemingly endless journey from the front door to the most remote room in the entire house; the room outside which, she now stood.

"Yes," stammered Patrice. "I remember you, but…"

"I knew you'd come back for me!" said the little girl, rushing out to wrap her arms around Patrice's waist and hugging her tightly.

Patrice was in an emotional state of shock as she fought to reconcile reality with the impossibility of the little girl clutching her tightly around the waist. Surely, she was dreaming, because none of this was even remotely possible yet, try as she might, she couldn't push the little girl's tangible presence back through the veil separating fact from fantasy.

As a child, Patrice was perpetually lonely within the walls of that house. There were no other children of her age within miles of her aunt's property, and from the time the school bus dropped her off at the main gate until it picked her up again on the next school day, she was for all intents and purposes... alone.

Nadine appeared a few days into Patrice's first summer school break while living at the estate. With her aunt's Tarot clients and the housekeepers being the sole exceptions, no one ever came into the house aside from her and Naomi and during those Tarot reading sessions, Patrice wasn't even allowed to leave her room upstairs.

While her aunt never charged for the readings, her clients never came to her empty-handed. Those who couldn't afford to pay in legal currency would often barter for her readings, exchanging items of value for Naomi's services. The items they offered were never appraised by Naomi prior to, or even after the Tarot readings, because the accuracy of her readings was karmically connected to the value of the objects presented by her clients. As a result, her assortment of odd yet valuable collectibles grew exponentially over the decades, filling the entire house with rare and intriguing objects of often unknown origin.

On one occasion, Patrice asked Aunt Naomi what she would do with all of the things people offered her in exchange for her readings. Naomi simply said, "When it's time to use them, they will present themselves to match the task at hand."

While the explanation left Patrice with more questions than answers, it did seem to at least satisfy her curiosity for the moment. A few weeks later, Patrice's English teacher gave them an optional assignment in which they would keep a journal of their activities covering their entire summer break. While the student diaries would remain private and confidential, they were intended to teach children the value of organizing their thoughts and documenting their ideas. She even explained how a young woman named Anne

Frank, had kept diaries which were subsequently read by millions of people from all around the world.

Patrice found the assignment to be an exciting one, and couldn't wait to start writing down her thoughts, experiences, and ideas inside her very own private journal. As soon as she came home from school, she excitedly asked Aunt Naomi for a notebook she could use as her journal.

"There are plenty of notepads and blank ledgers on the shelf in my study," said Naomi. "You can take one of them to use as your journal."

"Thank you, Aunt Naomi!" said Patrice, excitedly darting into the office. As she approached the bookshelf where her aunt kept the writing supplies, she spied a leather-bound book on the client chair across from her aunt's desk. Upon seeing it, she excitedly picked it up and flipped through the thick textured pages to make sure it was unused. "Can I have this one?" she yelled out the door of the study to her aunt.

Without even bothering to actually take a look at the journal Patrice had chosen, Naomi simply replied "As long as I haven't written anything inside it, you can take whichever one you'd like."

"Thank you, Aunt Naomi!" said Patrice, sprinting out of the office and up the stairs to her room. Once inside, she grabbed a pen from her nightstand and hopped onto her bed to begin her first journal entry.

Excitedly, while sprawled across the comforter, she wrote:

Dear Diary,

From now on, you will be my very best friend. I will tell you everything and share all of my secrets with you. Now that we're together, I will never have to be lonely again, because I will have you and you will have me... forever! 6-14-1985

After completing her first entry, she noticed a blank line inside the front cover at the very bottom of the page. It was preceded by a faded inscription, barely legible against the grain of the thick textured paper. Upon closer scrutiny, she deciphered the hidden text, reading it aloud. "Give me a name and speak it thrice, and I shall awaken when you sleep twice."

Over the next several hours, Patrice puzzled over a name for her journal, yet nothing she could think of seemed suitable for her new best friend. Suddenly, with her eyes closed, a name seemed to materialize clearly inside her mind. When she opened them and looked down at the page, she'd written the word, NADINE.

Surprised by the appearance of the name obviously written by her own hand, she spoke it aloud, saying "Nadine. Nadine? Nadine!" Smiling and nodding in approval, she added "Yes, I think that is perfect."

From that point forward, every entry was preceded by the salutation "Dear Nadine," and her attachment to the journal seemed to deepen and intensify with each passing day.

Now, as she stood frozen in the doorway with the arms of a mysterious young girl wrapped tightly around her waist, her sense of anxiety quickly dissipated. Taking her hand, the girl led Patrice into her former bedroom which was noticeably warmer than the rest of the house, including the hallway she'd just traversed.

When the door closed behind them, Patrice felt oddly... at home.

CHAPTER 2

"How are you even here?" asked Patrice, trying to piece the fragments of her childhood memories back together again.

"Because, you are here," Nadine replied. "I knew you'd come back for me, so I just waited."

Patrice remembered what appeared to be their first meeting, two days after beginning her journal. She'd written practically everything inside the diary—how it felt when she had to wait in her room, how she wished for another child to play with inside the massive house, and how happy she was to have discovered Nadine. After falling asleep with the journal clutched tightly to her, she awakened the next morning to find a girl her age sitting on the edge of the bed beside her.

"Good morning, Miss Patrice," said the smiling girl. "I'm Nadine."

From that day forward, she didn't even need to write inside her diary anymore. Everything she said to, or did with Nadine, automatically appeared inside the journal in her own handwriting followed by the current date. Best of all, she finally had the friend and playmate she longed for. Even though

Nadine couldn't physically leave the property, it never bothered Patrice who was happy to spend hours with her, exploring every nook and cranny of the massive estate.

 For years, she and Nadine were inseparable. Once the new school year began, Patrice constantly watched the clock, counting down the minutes until she could finally get home again. She would recount the day's experiences to her best friend as they sipped tea and ate the beignets Patrice brought upstairs from the kitchen. Each day, Nadine helped Patrice with her homework, and together they improved Patrice's grades and increased her overall knowledge of things she couldn't possibly have ever experienced first-hand.

 Following the completion of her homework, Patrice and Nadine would undertake the most amazing imaginary journeys, travelling to the furthest reaches of the earth and beyond. Each of those fantastic voyages would be diligently memorialized in great detail within the pages of the journal, which seemed impossible to fill. No matter the number of entries or the depth of their detail, the journal always had blank pages at the end; however, the journal itself, never seemed to increase in size or thickness.

As she sat there on the edge of the bed trying to reconstruct the puzzle before her, Nadine reached between the mattress and box-spring at the foot of the bed, withdrawing the journal from its decades-long hiding place. With a broad smile across her face, she reached out, presenting it to Patrice.

Cautiously, Patrice extended her hand accepting the journal. It felt remarkably light in comparison to its size and density, and as she flipped through the pages, she noticed they were each filled with text from their inside to their outside edges. They were all meticulously dated, beginning 6-14-1985 and ending abruptly on 8-24-1997—the day she departed Louisiana to attend the University of California at Los Angeles. Despite over twelve years of often lengthy daily entries, there were still a few blank pages remaining at the back of the journal.

Patrice clearly recalled the sadness she felt upon leaving Nadine behind; however, as the distance between them increased, the physical tug on her heartstrings decreased. By the time she reached Los Angeles, it had faded completely, all but erasing Nadine from her memory.

After years of living with Naomi, Patrice developed a natural curiosity for ancient cultures and rituals which was a deciding factor when she elected to pursue a master's degree in Anthropology. During her course of study, she was relentless in her search for answers which could explain the magic so skillfully wielded by her aunt. While many viewed Naomi as a witch, she saw herself as a spiritual healer helping people to understand the need for psychic cleansing and karmic balance. Often those who publicly rebuked her, would secretly appear on her doorstep seeking her advice days or even hours later. She never sent anyone away that came to her searching for answers, regardless of how they treated her in public. She believed good and evil were like opposing sides of the same coin, and it was up to each individual to choose which side of that coin they would put on display.

  As a child, Patrice was unaware of the discomfort her gift aroused in others and honestly didn't realize there was anything at all odd about it. Her abilities would manifest themselves only in times of great distress or perceived danger and were often highly volatile when they surfaced. The night she was deposited at Naomi's doorstep, Patrice had walked in on her mother and a "gentleman caller" believing he was attacking her. Her instinctive reaction snatched the man from her mother, flinging him across the room into the wall opposite the bed. By the time he regained consciousness, she'd spirited Patrice out of the filthy little apartment and into the backseat of her rusted AMC Pacer.

Naomi and Patrice never spoke of her mother, and after a few months she'd been permanently filed away in the annals of Patrice's long-forgotten memories. While Naomi never discouraged Patrice's gifts, neither did she encourage them, stating just as she had regarding the countless objects and items scattered throughout the enormous house, that when the need arose the appropriate gift would appear.

Although the price for living without fear of expressing her talents was the semi-isolation from other children of her age, the mere presence of Naomi seemed to be a moderating factor for Patrice. In the relative safety of the sprawling mansion, she gained the self-discipline she needed to control her overreactive tendencies, and after the manifestation of her living diary, Nadine, even Naomi's secluded estate seemed more of a haven than a prison.

During her childhood, she and Nadine had explored nearly every corner of the house. The only exceptions were Naomi's bedroom chamber adjacent to her study on the first floor, and the root cellar where Naomi kept her dry and canned goods, natural elixirs and healing potions, salted and smoked meats, and late-season fruits and vegetables.

The root cellar was off limits because the humidity inside needed to remain constant in order to prevent the food stored there from spoiling. Naomi's bedroom was off limits because it was her sanctuary. Like Patrice's bedroom upstairs, it had been spiritually cleansed and blessed and was a safe haven from any malevolent energies which could have attached themselves to the clients who visited the house.

Patrice's bedroom was located at the furthest possible point inside the house away from Naomi's study and bedroom chamber. While it could have been perceived as a means of keeping Patrice out of her hair during client sessions, it was actually done so the integrity of Patrice's sanctuary would also remain uncorrupted. Once her room had been cleansed and blessed, even Aunt Naomi never entered it again.

Patrice spoke often of Nadine, who was treated by Naomi and the housekeepers as her imaginary friend. Even when describing the fanciful journeys and adventures the two of them had undertaken, the adults in the room never seemed to take her seriously, smiling and nodding politely while attributing Patrice's colorful yarns to the overactive imagination of a lonely young girl. Of course, neither Patrice nor Nadine required encouragement or confirmation from others to validate their friendship, and despite the occasional raised eyebrows and confused expressions on the faces of others, their connection continued unabated.

As Patrice aged and matured, Nadine did not. She remained the ten-year-old girl Patrice's imagination had originally conjured. With each passing year, Nadine became more like a little sister than a best friend and, as young teenage women are want to do, Patrice increasingly sought the company of girls her own age. Even though Nadine remained her closest confidant, the size and number of entries to her diary steadily decreased until the final entry on 8-24-1997.

Sitting there in the bedroom of her childhood, Patrice's recollections of past events were revived in vivid detail while scanning through the pages of her journal. As a child, she'd simply accepted facts as they presented themselves. Nadine was real, the journal pages refilled themselves, and whatever she and Nadine did together, was automatically added to the journal. Having had no one around her to tell her anything to the contrary, she accepted all of those things as normal.

It seemed odd to Patrice that her memories of Nadine had been so completely and effectively suppressed during her absence. Based on the sheer number of intricately detailed journal entries, the memories of Nadine should have been indelibly branded into her brain's hippocampus. Despite that fact, Patrice couldn't remember even a single instance in which she'd missed Nadine or even thought of her after arriving at UCLA. Even her extensive field studies and published essays dealing with north American spiritual and supernatural culture, never jogged the memories of either the journal or the manifestation of Nadine as an entity; something which should have set off every alarm bell in her head.

She continued reading through the journal entries as Nadine sat patiently beside her on the edge of the bed. It was almost as if she were "paused", awaiting further instructions from Patrice. Each time she looked over at Nadine, the little girl would immediately light up in anticipation, and when her focus returned to the journal, Nadine seemed to return to sleep mode.

What she *had* recognized immediately, was that the physical journal she now held in her hands was no ordinary diary. It was a grimoire—a book traditionally used to document magic spells and incantations. Upon naming it, Patrice had awakened the soul of the grimoire and her deep longing for a playmate fueled by her childish imagination, had actually called Nadine into existence.

After nearly an hour spent reacquainting herself with her childhood, it was obvious she'd barely even scratched the surface of the journal's contents. She hadn't even made it through the second page before fatigue set in. The cumulative effects of a full day spent cataloging a veritable warehouse of mystery objects, the sudden reappearance of Nadine, and the inviting comfort of the bed beneath her, made the lure of a nap much too tempting to resist.

Upon closing the journal, she looked over at the bed beside her. Nadine was gone but Patrice was far too exhausted to puzzle over yet another mystery. She kicked off her shoes and pulled the comforter at the foot of the bed up over her before falling into a deep, much-needed sleep.

As she slept, Nadine reappeared, gently removing the journal from Patrice's hands, and returning it to its proper place between the mattress and box spring at the foot of the bed.

Standing beside the bed, Nadine smiled and whispered, "Welcome home, Miss Patrice. You've been gone for far, far too long." With a final glance, she walked across the room to the light switch near the bedroom door. When she flipped it to the OFF position, the room was plunged into darkness and Nadine, once again, vanished.

CHAPTER 3

The next morning, Patrice awoke with a start, curiously looking around the room, not quite sure of what to expect. The shoes she'd haphazardly kicked off before falling asleep were now placed neatly together beside the bed, precisely next to the spot on the floor where her feet landed naturally each day when she arose. Just as she began to consider the improbability of the events from the prior evening, Nadine swept into the room; all smiles and brimming with joy.

"Good morning, Miss Patrice!" she said melodically, gliding across the room as if floating on air. Reaching the window, she pulled aside the heavy drapes to reveal bright sunlight flooding the room and painting the deep green canvas of the Shreveport countryside.

"Good morning, Nadine," replied Patrice, well beyond any thread of doubt that the girl was, in fact, real.

"Barely, sleepyhead," replied Nadine. "It's nearly noon. I thought you were going to sleep the entire day away."

"Hardly," said Patrice. "I have far too much to do today, and my sleep allotment expired hours ago."

"Then let's get started," said Nadine. "What are we doing today?"

Suddenly, Patrice remembered Nadine's infectious enthusiasm—the same enthusiasm that had landed Patrice in hot water with Aunt Naomi and her housekeepers on more than one occasion. Even so, whether it was her homework, her daily chores, or their concocted schemes to get even with the bullies who taunted her at school, everything seemed to fall into place much faster when she and Nadine worked together. Considering the daunting task ahead of her, a little help wouldn't necessarily be a bad thing.

Eyeing Nadine as if pondering her options, she finally nodded, saying "Well, I do need to get everything in the house cleaned up and cataloged, and judging by the tiny dent I made in that project yesterday... I could definitely use some help."

"Great!" exclaimed Nadine, grabbing Patrice's hand and pulling her excitedly towards the bedroom door. "Come on then. It'll be just like before you left."

When they reached the ground floor, Patrice was surprised to find the room in a much-improved state over the one in which she'd left it. Her empty water bottles and leftovers from the previous day had been cleared away, the luggage from her SUV was now inside, placed in graduating size order near the closet beneath the stairs, and even the dust-bunnies and cobwebs so abundant upon Patrice's arrival, were gone.

Not surprisingly, the two of them worked together like a well-oiled machine, quickly accomplishing in a few hours what Patrice would have needed a week to get done. By sunset, Patrice knew more about her aunt's bizarre collection of antique curiosities, than she'd learned in the twelve years spent living under the same roof with them. Evidently, Naomi's clients took karma quite seriously because, with very few exceptions, everything they cataloged was either extremely rare, or extremely valuable, or both.

While Nadine's stature was that of a ten-year-old, the pool of her knowledge was deep and mysterious. She seemed instinctively able to divine the origins and purposes of nearly every object they came across—some of which, were hundreds of years old. The more objects they discovered, the more evident the depth of Nadine's knowledge became.

After wrapping up their final entry on the ground floor, Patrice decided it was time to call it a night. Before heading up the stairs, she finished off the take-out from the previous evening and cleared away the boxes and eating utensils in the kitchen. Satisfied with their efforts of the day, she turned off the lights on the ground floor and headed towards the stairs Nadine had ascended several minutes earlier.

On the stairs, it occurred to Patrice that the unnatural cold which seemed to fill the entire house the day before, had now receded upward to the second floor. The effect was like climbing into a much higher altitude, but as she passed beyond the landing leading up to the third floor, the cold seemed to dissipate, and the temperature normalized. When she entered her bedroom at the end of the hallway, Nadine was there waiting for her, sitting on the edge of the bed with the journal on the comforter beside her.

"I'm really glad you came back, Patrice," said Nadine. "It's wonderful that we're together again."

"I'd nearly forgotten how great a team we were," said Patrice.

"We *are*..." interjected Nadine. "We *are* a great team. Even a lifetime of separation couldn't change that."

As she sat there on the bed, Patrice couldn't help but notice the similarities between the two of them. At that age, she and Nadine could easily have been mistaken for sisters, if not outright twins. Even now, Nadine could easily have passed as her daughter, *if* anyone aside from Patrice had actually been able to see her. Taking a spot beside her on the bed, Patrice picked up the journal, curiously opening it and skipping to the final entry. It was dated one day earlier and neatly penned in her own handwriting. Even the subtle changes to her writing style over the years hadn't been missed by Nadine's highly detailed accounting of events.

With a knowing smile, Patrice laid back across the bed to continue reading from the journal. Each subsequent entry revealed more and more of her life's story as a child growing up on the outskirts of Shreveport, Louisiana. Some entries were of typical episodes experienced by girls her age in cities and countries all over the world. Others were more detailed in nature and included poetry and prose not typical for a child of that age. In fact, the further along she progressed, the more evident her level of maturity became, and like most teenage girls, for a time she'd seemed to have developed a bit of a mean streak. While her poems and childish incantations were more like the fledgling attempts of an amateur, either by skill or by blind luck, they had been effective.

One incident in particular suddenly crystalized in her memory. She was twelve years old at the time, and a boy a bit older than Patrice seemed to have taken a shine to her. Unfortunately, her list of natural talents didn't include tact, and her boisterous kneejerk rejection left him angry and humiliated. Following the incident, he used every possible opportunity to embarrass her and tarnish the remaining fragments of her reputation. With the abundant selection of protection spells in Naomi's library, she could easily have prevented him from even coming close to her. Unfortunately, after months of relentless badgering, he'd pushed Patrice beyond her breaking point.

With Nadine's help, Patrice crafted a vengeance spell that would reflect the ill intent he hurled at her, back toward him in equal measure. The simple incantation read:

    For those who harbor ill intent, let evil follow pathways bent.

    Return to those who wish me ill, the outcome of their evil will.

The following morning, Thomas McGee could barely contain his excitement. The prank he'd planned for Patrice, would be legendary. He fidgeted the entire day, counting down the minutes until the three o'clock bell. When it rang, Thomas immediately sprang from his seat and made a beeline for the exit doors. That morning before school, he'd discovered an unused cherry bomb left over from Memorial Day, and hastily devised a plan to use it against Patrice. He'd wait until she exited the side door then sneak up behind her, light the cherry bomb, and drop it into her backpack. He could just imagine the look on her face when it exploded and she began flapping about hysterically, trying to rid herself of it—to say nothing of the confetti it would create from the books and folders inside her backpack.

The school bus loading zone was buzzing with students when Patrice came through the door. As planned, Thomas slipped up behind her following quietly. When he was within reach of her backpack, he pulled the cherry bomb from his pocket and lit the fuse. It exploded immediately, sending kids scattering in every direction. When bus stop monitors converged on the scene, they discovered Thomas writhing on the ground in agony, clutching what remained of his mutilated left hand. It was the last prank he ever attempted to pull on Patrice or anyone else for that matter. In fact, he didn't return to school for the remainder of the year.

While Patrice realized she wasn't responsible for Thomas's reckless actions, she did feel horrible about the severity of his injuries. Nadine's granular detail in documenting the events of that day and those that followed, served as a potent reminder of the dangers associated with even the most innocent use of spells and incantations.

Although Naomi never said a word about the matter, her sense of awareness would certainly not have missed the aura of an incantation formed within the walls of her own house. It took only a passing glance in Patrice's direction for Naomi to convey that message, and even without her direct admonishment, the message was clearly delivered and received.

Since returning to the estate, Patrice's connection to both the house and Nadine had grown noticeably stronger, and after a night spent tossing and turning, she could feel there was turbulence within those enchanted walls. It was as if the recent flurry of activity had awakened something which did not wish to be disturbed. It was an old energy… possibly an ancient one, and it felt to Patrice as if it were angry.

Whatever was causing the energy disturbances in the house must have arrived after Patrice left for college. Despite a number of rumors to the contrary, the Lafleur estate had always been a place of light and joyful energy. In fact, it seemed immune to the tensions plaguing Shreveport during the economic recession from the mid-1980s to the early 1990s. However, since the actual house sat back away from the main road, obscured by century-old oak trees and a high wrought-iron gate, it was often the target of ominous gossip and rampant speculation. Nevertheless, for a growing child, the Lafleur estate was a wonderful place to live and learn, and Patrice had never felt anything but love and positivity while living there.

As always, after falling asleep with her journal, she awakened to find it had once again been returned to its proper location between the mattress and box spring at the foot of the bed. Slipping into a morning robe and the house shoes at her bedside, she left the room and headed down the stairs. At the second story landing, she paused to look down the long dark hallway to her left. There in the shadowy recesses near the end of the corridor, Nadine stood with her back to Patrice staring at the rustic steel door that sealed the entrance to the foreboding room.

Cautiously, she approached from behind slowly extending her hand towards the little girl's shoulder. Upon touching her, the girl who quickly turned to face her was *not* Nadine! Her face was old and wizened, twisted into gruesome and clearly demonic features with sunken eyes as black as obsidian. The voice emanating from the disfigured old crone was reminiscent of fingernails dragging slowly across a chalkboard as she shrieked, "You do not belong here!"

Gasping out loud, Patrice stumbled backwards, crashing through the handrail that was suddenly right behind her. The domed ceiling above her zoomed further and further away as she plummeted downward, awaiting the sudden deceleration of impact against the unforgiving marble floor below.

Patrice bolted upright in the bed to find Nadine standing right next to her. The drapes were already open, and sunlight flooded into the room, scattering the remnants of her nightmarish vision. Within the space of a few seconds, the dread saturating the room had been wholly replaced by Nadine's near effervescent optimism.

"Good morning, Miss Patrice!" she said. "Breakfast is ready, and I brewed a fresh pot of coffee for you."

"Nadine, somehow you're always a step ahead of me." said Patrice.

"Let's just say, I'm a quick study," Nadine replied. "Besides, I've got years of notes I can refer to and, as you know, past is prologue."

Nodding in acknowledgement, Patrice dressed and followed Nadine down the stairs. The cold spot in the house was now densely concentrated on the westernmost wing of the second floor, and as they passed the second-floor landing, Nadine nonchalantly said "We're not ready yet," before continuing down the stairs and into the kitchen.

In the breakfast nook, Nadine had placed a basket of freshly prepared beignets and a cup of hot coffee with milk on the table for Patrice. For so many years, that nook had been the center of Patrice's childhood. She and Naomi began each day enjoying breakfast together at the little table. Unlike the studio apartment she shared with her mother, there was always food either cooking on the stove, being warmed inside the oven, prepared, and covered on the countertops, or stored inside the refrigerator. Much of the improvement in Patrice's grades was due to her ability to then focus on something other than the gnawing hunger in her belly.

Naomi and Patrice's mother, Juliette, had both been given an excellent foundation upon which to build their futures. Juliette was the older of the two, having been born only a few minutes before Naomi, her fraternal twin sister. As young children, they'd been inseparable; however, upon reaching puberty their paths diverged sharply. Where Naomi had developed an early fascination for her grandmother's holistic approaches to life, health, and happiness, and was anxious to unlock the secrets of the natural energy surrounding them, Juliette wanted nothing more than to escape the secluded estate that she viewed as a prison.

Just as it had been with Patrice, there were no other children living within a mile of the secluded estate. More specifically in Juliette's view, there were no boys. Where Naomi's pubescent energy blossomed into a deep connection to nature and the powerful forces it harbored, in stark contrast, Juliette's attention was drawn irresistibly to men, and her desire to *be* desired completely eclipsed everything outside that narrow prism of focus for her.

Neither of the sisters had ever been married; however, the reasons for their perpetual single statuses were again, vastly different. Naomi's attraction to the unbridled energy of the universe proved to be more seductive than the charms of any man could ever have been. In contrast, Juliette forcefully threw herself at any man who showed even the slightest interest in her. Her promiscuity was well-known, and the hypocritical men who laid with her in the darkness, shunned her in the light of day.

After losing both parents in an automobile accident shortly before the girls' eighteenth birthday, they were raised to adulthood by their grandmother, Marie Lafleur. Naomi's relationship to Marie and the Lafleur estate had always been close; however, Juliette was anxious to put as much distance as possible between herself, the estate, *and* her grandmother. Upon Marie's passing three years later, the estate was settled, and Juliette took her portion of the inheritance in cash. Within days, she left the property without ever looking back.

Between the two sisters, Patrice was the only descendant and while she was Juliette's daughter, her character and the gifts which began to manifest within her, were much more suited to a life with Naomi than to the constant uncertainty and repeated upheavals which punctuated the life of her biological mother. Although the circumstances surrounding her arrival at the Lafleur estate were far from ideal, living there with Naomi had undoubtedly changed the trajectory of her life for the better.

Now, as the sole heir to the Lafleur estate, Patrice was able to use her educational background in anthropology to research and better understand the veritable treasure trove of relics that Grandma Marie, and Aunt Naomi had acquired over the course of their lives dating back more than a century. Thanks to Nadine, after only two days of diligent research, she'd identified more anthropologically significant items here, than she had during nearly two decades of field work in remote locations around the globe... and she'd yet to even explore the mysteries behind the iron door on the second floor.

CHAPTER 4

Patrice had been studying ancient cultures in the middle east when she received notification of her Aunt's passing. As Naomi's sole living relative, it had taken nearly four years for the attorney to track her down, and once he did it was still no easy task for him to convince her she'd inherited the Lafleur estate. Even after the first full week there, it was difficult for her to comprehend the full weight of that inheritance.

Since her arrival, she'd only left the estate on one occasion, driving to Shreveport to purchase food, personal hygiene products, and cleaning supplies. After living in Los Angeles for more than twenty years, visiting Shreveport was like stepping backwards into a time capsule. The population had actually shrunken since the time she'd live there, and the things that were old then, were older now. Otherwise, not much had changed.

Having emptied the contents of the trailer, she first located a store where she could drop it off before continuing on to the supermarket. At the drop-off point, she never left her vehicle, nor did she need to in order to recognize the man unhitching the trailer and signing off on her rental return document. Although his bearded face and greasy hair were in no way unique to Shreveport, the mutilated left hand with its missing index and middle fingers made it clear to her that she was once again dealing with Thomas McGee.

Pretending not to notice as he checked the trailer and initialed the return document, it was definitely an uncomfortable moment for Patrice when he handed her the customer copy through the lowered window, saying "Have a nice day, Miss Lafleur."

"Thank you, Sir," said Patrice with a smile before raising the window and driving out of the parking lot. Once underway again, she realized her pulse was racing. After all, what were the odds of meeting the one person she'd spent most of her childhood avoiding, during her very first trip into Shreveport?

That thought accompanied her during the entire shopping excursion. Thomas had given her no reason to feel as uneasy as she did, but her paranoia persisted until the gates at the Lafleur estate closed behind her again. For the time being, she would put the incident out of her mind, but perhaps there was something she could do to help him in some small way. Time would certainly tell.

Back inside the house, Patrice was mentally preparing for her next project while she and Nadine stored the products and supplies, she'd purchased. It was something she'd been mentally preparing for since the day of her arrival; however, she still felt a bit apprehensive at the prospect of entering Naomi's personal sanctuary.

After bathing and cleansing her body with handmade ritual soap made from frankincense, myrrh, lavender, and sandalwood, she slipped into a white robe woven from natural unbleached cotton. In the study outside Naomi's bedroom chamber, Patrice cleansed her aura and spirit through hours of meditation and prayer, and by the time she entered the room it was late afternoon.

Immediately upon crossing the threshold, Patrice could sense Naomi's magnificent aura. The warmth and security she felt was amazing and beautiful, and seemed to welcome her into its embrace. Allowing herself a moment to bask in the sense of overwhelming love permeating the very fabric of the sanctuary, Patrice's sense of apprehension evaporated, dissipating completely within seconds.

Ahead of her was a wooden pedestal upon which a heavy ledger was placed. Its energy seemed to reach out to Patrice, beckoning her to come closer. Protruding from it like a bookmark, was a legal-sized envelope with Patrice's name written along the visible edge. It was approximately two-thirds of the way through the heavy leather book, but before proceeding to the pages marked by the envelope, Patrice opened it to the very first entry. It was dated 11-23-1642. The ledger in front of her was a grimoire, and it was over 370 years old.

The significance of the moment was not lost on Patrice, and with trembling hands, she opened the journal to the pages marked by the envelope. The entry read:

> My Dearest Patrice,
>
> My time as guardian of the gateway will soon draw to an end, and you, my treasured child, are destined to assume stewardship of this monumental responsibility. Although this revelation may feel overwhelming to you as you read this letter, in your heart, you know this has always been your destiny.
>
> Ours is not an easy pathway. It is fraught with obstacles and the disdain of those who cannot comprehend the magnitude of our calling. Still, you must be steadfast and resolute in your role as guardian. Help anyone and everyone who

presents themselves to you, as the energy of the gateway is there for the good of all mankind—even those who may speak ill of you. Forgive them and help them anyway.

Above all, resist any temptations to use the energy of the gateway for the advancement of your personal desires, for that is the path to your own destruction. The energy of the portal is divine in nature, and as you provide for others, so shall the portal provide for you.

As I sought to impress upon you as a child, good and evil are two sides of the same coin and it is up to each individual to choose which side they reveal. It was the love and kindness in your heart that shaped the destiny which brought you to this moment in time, and that same love and kindness will guide you in the fulfillment of your duties.

Your precious Nadine will continue to assist you in channeling your energy, just as she has done since you discovered her in my study, so many years ago. When the need arose, she was the tool that presented itself to you, and she will be a powerful ally in your role as guardian of the portal. When in doubt, trust her judgement for she is the very reflection of your inner good and will lead you to the light, even when your path must cross through darkness.

The vast knowledge of your sisters can be found within the pages of this journal, just as the records of your Nadine shall continue herein, as my chapter closes, and your chapter begins. Treat the journal as a living thing, and the knowledge you seek will always be revealed to you.

My sanctuary is now your sanctuary. Blessed be your path as a guardian, and always remember that I love you.

Naomi Lafleur, 10-22-2014.

Patrice stood motionless as she absorbed the posthumous message from her aunt. After a moment, she opened the envelope and read the notarized legal document confirming all of the information provided by Naomi's attorney. After reading it, she placed it back inside the envelope and turned to find Nadine standing behind her, holding Patrice's journal.

"It's time we moved," said Nadine, stepping closer. She was no longer a little girl, but her brightly glowing aura was as joyous as it had always been.

"You've changed," said Patrice with an approving smile.

"*You've* changed," said Nadine. "I am simply a reflection of who you've become."

Raising the journal, Nadine presented it to Patrice one final time. Patrice took it and placed it on top of the open pages following Naomi's letter inside the ancient grimoire. The two ledgers instantly melded into one another, integrating Patrice's records into the much larger journal resting on the pedestal.

Looking at Nadine, Patrice said "Well, it looks like we're about to embark on a new journey together."

"The journey began the moment you came through that front door one week ago," Nadine replied. Looking around Patrice's new sanctuary and bedroom chamber, she added "I guess now there is only one room left to explore."

"Soon," replied Patrice. "First, I'd like to learn as much as I can about what to expect behind that door, but somehow, I feel confident the answers are already here," she added, patting the thick leather cover of the grimoire. As she turned to face the pedestal again, Nadine retreated into the study closing the door behind her.

Speaking softly to herself, Patrice said "So... Let's see what you can tell me about the portal."

When she reached toward the journal, the pages flipped themselves as if moved by the airflow of an oscillating fan. Once they'd settled near the beginning of the book, to Patrice's surprise, the information displayed was all related to the discovery of the portal and the energy emanating from it. The location was discovered by the Native American Caddo Indian tribe, centuries prior to the first ledger entry inside the grimoire. It was considered sacred ground and protected by a succession of their female spiritual leaders, who would perform ghost dances to help the living connect with the dead.

Their first contact with Europeans came in 1542 when the peaceful tribe was attacked and slaughtered by a Spanish expeditionary force. Shortly thereafter, religious missionaries arrived carrying the germs which caused the smallpox epidemic that decimated the Caddo's population. As other Native American populations were driven from their ancestral lands in vast regions of what is now known as Louisiana, stewardship of the portal was passed to a descendant of the fragmented Acolapissa Tribe: Meaning "those who listen and see." During that period, vast areas within the

Texas-Louisiana region were annexed by European settlers whose very presence brought diseases that made inhabitation by indigenous peoples, impossible.

In 1640, the land surrounding the portal was purchased by a wealthy French nobleman named Francois Lafleur, who had the sprawling estate built before permanently migrating from Normandy to the Louisiana territory with his wife, Marguerite. Shortly after moving into the residence, Marguerite sensed the presence of the immense energy field hovering at the second floor just beyond the outer wall of the original building, and in 1642, she became the first European to serve as guardian of the portal. She immediately began researching and documenting her findings in the pages of the grimoire she named Elenore, and when the house was partially destroyed by fire following a lightning strike, she had the walls of the room extended to encompass the portal's entryway when the damaged wing was rebuilt.

Not long after that, Louisiana became an administrative district of France, and the Lafleur family name was held in high esteem throughout the region. Even after generations of skirmishes, changes of allegiance, revolution, and civil war, the Lafleur estate remained untouched and undamaged by external forces, regardless of how close they might have come to the property's perimeter.

The portal, as implied by its name, was an opening into another realm—one through which energy could both be withdrawn or sent into. The guardians controlled the flow of spiritual traffic in both directions by using the energy it emitted to bind malevolent forces and banish them into the realm beyond the portal. As long as a guardian stood watch at the estate, the energy they channeled served as an impenetrable barrier for entities seeking to escape that nether region. Although other methods could create temporary barriers, the buildup of malevolent energy in the absence of a guardian would eventually become powerful enough to push through them. Their emergence was most often preceded by unexpected cold spots and power fluctuations as entities harvested energy from this dimension to increase their power in another one. As they grew stronger, the unnatural chill would spread until it reached a more powerful source of fuel, the ultimate source being the sun. While those malevolent spirits could not exist in direct sunlight, the cold tendrils they extended served as conduits transferring energy back to the entities inside the portal.

The portal itself, was the source of the guardians' power, which they channeled through either a sacred object or spirit animal familiar to them. For Native American Indians, bears, foxes, and wolves were the most common spirit animals; however, large birds of prey such as hawks, falcons, owls, and eagles were also used. European guardians traditionally focused their energy through objects such as crystal orbs, enchanted wands, animal bones, Ouija boards, and as in Naomi's case, Tarot cards.

Patrice was unique, in that she was the only guardian in recorded history to have caused the physical manifestation of her own channel. Her emergence had been foreseen by past guardians and was clearly documented inside the pages of the ancient ledger. When she arrived, her mere presence was enough to weaken the malevolent spirits amassed on the other side of the portal, and the longer she remained, the more of her energy filled the vacuum left by Naomi. The steady retreat of the supernatural chill and ever-increasing brightness of the interior lighting were indications that Patrice's command of the portal was imminent.

When she finally emerged from the trance-like study session, hours had passed, and the sun had long set. Upon emerging from the sanctuary, she felt energized and empowered, and ready to assume the mantle of stewardship for the Lafleur family bloodline. Taking a seat behind the heavy wooden desk in the study, Patrice exhaled deeply, and her thoughts turned to the iron door sealing the gateway on the second floor. With Nadine's presence to concentrate and focus her energy, she was destined to become the most powerful guardian to have ever held watch over the portal.

Now... She was ready.

CHAPTER 5

Following her first full night in the new bedroom chamber, Patrice awoke refreshed and energized. Nadine had already opened the curtains and placed her slippers next to the bed, and the inviting aroma of freshly brewed coffee wafted across the distance from the kitchen into the sanctuary.

"Good morning, Miss Patrice," came the melodic greeting from a beautifully evolved Nadine. Her mature countenance was as lovely as Patrice would have expected, and closely mirrored her own. The delightful yellow aura that surrounded her as a child, had also brightened and was now nearly white, standing out even against the intensity of the sundrenched bedroom chamber.

As Patrice walked past the pedestal on her way into the kitchen, a quick glance at the grimoire confirmed her expectation that the prior day's events had already been added to the journal in her own handwriting and dated accordingly.

"Whatever would I do without you, Nadine?" Patrice asked, rhetorically.

"I have no idea," replied Nadine with a smile. "because I wouldn't be around to notice."

Acknowledging her logic with a smile, Patrice was happy to see that Nadine's senses of humor and irony were still firmly in place. However, the answer did remind Patrice of a question that had been nagging at her for a few days by then. As she sat down at the table in the breakfast nook, she asked "Why couldn't I remember you while I was in college?"

"It was for your own protection," Nadine replied. "The temptation to rely on your gifts and my knowledge in earning your degree would have been too great, and your achievements would have forever been called into question. By entirely removing me from the equation, your accomplishments are now irrefutable. Besides, using spells and incantations for your own personal benefit creates unpredictable karmic backlash."

"You know me well," said Patrice. "There were times I'd have done nearly anything to make it through my classes and seminars. All I really wanted to participate in were the field research trips."

"That comes as no surprise to me," said Nadine. "You have always been an explorer, and fortunately for you, there is still much left to be discovered."

Nodding in silent agreement, Patrice finished her breakfast of sliced fruits and melons and after a second cup of coffee, she arose and returned to her sanctuary to bathe and get dressed. Wrapping up her morning routine, she entered the study where she spent the next hour in prayer and deep meditation. The task ahead of her was an important one, and she would need to be spiritually cleansed and emotionally prepared to face it.

Upon leaving the study, she walked directly over to the stairs where Nadine was patiently waiting for her. At the second floor, they proceeded down the long corridor together, stopping in front of the iron door. While the door itself seemed to be radiating cold air towards them, the corridor itself, was no longer affected by it. On the floor near the threshold, Patrice noticed a thick line drawn across the hallway from wall to wall using salted chalk.

Both salt and iron are effective tools in preventing the advance of malevolent spirits beyond areas to which they've been confined. Salted chalk is also quite handy for use in drawing glyphs and occult binding symbols which further reinforce protective barriers erected to deter evil spirits.

Patrice could feel the immense energy of the portal encircling them. To her left, Nadine's aura was glowing bright white as she absorbed and focused it into a concentrated mass. When Patrice raised her right hand opening her fingers as she pushed towards the iron door, Nadine's right hand grasped her left wrist, channeling an unfathomable amount of energy through Patrice's body and into an intense pulse-like wave. Focusing that energy on the cold metal door, her body was trembling from exertion as it finally began to move. The massive door travelled nearly two feet inward before it finally cleared the doorjamb on the inside of the room by just a crack. Patrice realized that there was neither a lock nor a latch on the door, and that the sheer weight of it would have made it nearly impossible to move by hand.

    Patrice redoubled her efforts, and as the door slowly opened, more and more of the room beyond it was revealed, bathed in a glowing bluish-white light. The oxidized iron walls, ceiling, and floor inside were covered in ancient symbols and words written in a language long dead and forgotten. At the very center of the room, seemingly suspended in mid-air, was a narrow chasm so dark that even the blinding glow of the surrounding room could not illuminate it. It was like peering into a miniature black hole so powerful, even light could not escape it.

Patrice could sense the rage of the legion of entities amassed behind the black veil as she focused her energy directly on the portal, forcing them deeper into the abyss. Although the gateway had been unguarded for nearly four years, Naomi's spiritual preparations had been powerful enough to prevent them from escaping their supernatural prison. Nadine's presence effectively augmented the measures taken by Naomi. Her indominable positivity had created an insurmountable pocket of resistance which, combined with the protective energy of the grimoire within Naomi's sanctuary, created powerful barriers at each end of the house, effectively preventing them from spreading beyond the walls of the estate.

After several minutes of bombarding the gateway with energy drawn from the portal itself, Patrice felt the resistance beyond the black veil evaporating. As the legion's resistance faded, her power increased tilting the advantage decidedly in her favor. A few seconds later, the portal closed, and the malevolent energy disappeared entirely.

Suddenly, the atmosphere around them felt light and airy and the remaining tendrils of cold quickly warmed and vanished. Patrice lowered her hand and Nadine released her wrist as they stepped across the threshold into the now peaceful room.

As an added precaution, Patrice cleansed the room with smoldering sage before blessing and sealing it against all malevolent spirits. When they returned to the hallway outside the door, the disturbances polluting the energy inside the house were gone without a trace.

Raising her right hand again, this time she pulled it towards her while closing her fingers into a fist. The massive iron door swung towards them, closing easily and without a sound.

Downstairs in her study, Patrice was tired but pleased that the spiritual balance within the house had been restored. As a guardian, her presence within the vicinity of the portal would prevent future accumulations of negative energy originating from inside the gateway; however, now that the portal's integrity had been restored, it was only a matter of time before those suffering souls seeking to rid themselves of their own malevolent spiritual hitchhikers would begin to arrive.

The door leading inside Patrice's study was immediately to the left of the front door after entering the house. This was important, because clients could visit that room without having to traipse through the entire house to get there.

Contrary to most of her clients' expectations, the room was bright and spacious. In fact, it looked more like an accountant's office than it did a place to rid oneself of malevolent spirits. Like Naomi, Patrice was also much different than the mental stereotypes expected of one who deals with evil spirits and occult energies. In a word, she was beautiful.

Even while attending UCLA, and later when working with field expeditionary teams in often abhorrent and austere conditions, it was difficult for others to look beyond the obvious distraction of her stunning appearance. It didn't matter whether she was analyzing the contents of petrified human feces or crawling through the narrow entryways of ancient South American burial chambers, looming above it all was the stark realization that no matter what she did, she never looked anything other than perfect.

Patrice, while as aware of her genetically inherited beauty as any other attractive woman, never viewed her outward appearance as collateral she could use as leverage to have her way or to get what she wanted. The way her mother allowed men to use and abuse her because of her incessant need to be complimented and desired, was one of the few things Patrice could remember about her. Even a blindingly beautiful woman like Juliette becomes tiresome and undesirable once someone realizes she's an emotional vampire, taking but never contributing, and constantly in need of praise and adoration. Patrice was determined *never* to venture down that self-destructive path.

Despite her lack of intention, both men and women found it difficult *not* to desire her. The more unapproachable she attempted to make herself, the more determined people around her would become in seeking her affection. As a result, much of her work and scientific analysis was done in solitude, communicating with peers and contemporaries in the fields of anthropology and archeology via email and direct messaging.

Within a few short years, her published papers and field study memoires were required reading in research laboratories, universities, and other institutions of higher learning around the world. Although her long-time publisher and editorial advisor assured her that he could boost her book sales and public appearance income by adding a photograph to her bio, she refused, insisting that her research and findings must be able to stand on their merits alone. Even so, the royalties from her published works continued to provide a substantial income for Patrice up to that day.

In 2014, she received a personal invitation from a colleague working at a newly discovered archeological dig site in the middle east. Based on his findings, the relics unearthed were of a civilization previously unknown, and he was seeking her expertise in identifying and running to ground, their potential origins. Her curiosity got the better of her, and five days later, she was landing in the kingdom of Jordan to join Professor Liam McKenna's dig at a remote location in the Jordanian Desert.

His team of handpicked professionals were so focused on the task at hand, they hardly even noticed Patrice... something that she greatly appreciated. After two years of painstakingly detailed work, the team had made a number of groundbreaking discoveries, and could confirm that the relics they'd uncovered so far, predated even those of Petra and Jerash.

Due to the length of time spent working the site together, Patrice and Liam developed remarkably close professional and personal relationships and, unexpected by either of them, they fell in love. Liam was the first person she'd ever known who accepted the fact that her professional achievements were the foundation of her success. On the flip side, Liam found that

Patrice's passion for discovery rivaled his own, actually matching him step for step. Once they entered each other's orbits, the gravity of their attraction was inevitable.

Their relationship, while solid, was also flexible. The nature of their professions necessarily meant they would face long-distance separations, but the depth of their feeling for one another kept them connected, regardless of the geographical distance between them. In fact, when the courier finally delivered the message from Naomi's attorney, Liam encouraged her to return to Shreveport in order to put the outstanding affairs of the Lafleur estate in order. Once he'd wrapped up the legal transfer of the dig site's research and discoveries to the Jordan Museum, he would join Patrice and assist her in determining the origins of the curious relics in her family's collection of artifacts.

Patrice had been quite open with Liam regarding her family history, wanting to put it all out there before things got too serious between them. Surprisingly, he was completely receptive regarding Naomi's gift as a spiritual guide and counselor. For Liam, it was perplexing that the need for spiritual cleansing was viewed so negatively in the United States—especially since it's a country founded on religious freedom. The thought of treating non-Christian spiritual leaders as pariahs struck him as hypocritical, and he welcomed the opportunity to experience it firsthand.

Patrice hadn't spoken with Liam since her arrival in Shreveport, due to the remote location of the dig site in Jordan. Considering the events of the past week, she would certainly have a lot to discuss with him. Hopefully, he'd be sitting down when they spoke.

CHAPTER 6

Liam was actually lying down when he called. He'd only been home for an hour or so, having just put a twenty-hour flight from Amman, Jordan to Glasgow, Scotland behind him. Even though he was physically drained, he wanted to speak with Patrice before falling into the semi-coma his body would need in order to regenerate.

"Liam!" exclaimed Patrice upon recognizing his name flashing on her smartphone's caller ID. "I am so glad you called!"

"I got in about an hour ago and wanted to call you before I punch out for a spell," said Liam with his unmistakable Scottish accent. "Somehow, the Jordanian Desert isn't quite the same without you."

"I suppose I'll take that as a compliment," said Patrice with a smile.

"As well you should!" Liam replied. "I could have spent the rest of my life there before you left. Afterwards, it was just a bunch of sand separating me from you."

"Well, there's still the tiny matter of that thing we call the Atlantic between us," giggled Patrice. "But we *are* getting closer."

"It's but a pond," said Liam. "I've got to check in with the university tomorrow morning, but after that, I'll be on my way to you, even if I have to swim."

"That's very sweet of you," said Patrice. "But I'd prefer you fly, just the same."

"Already booked," said Liam. "I must be madly in love with you, to brave two different twenty-hour flights within four days, but... the heart wants what it wants."

"I wish I could say you don't need to put yourself through so much trouble for me," Patrice replied. "But, for purely selfish reasons, I insist that you do. I love you, and I miss you so much already, sweetheart."

"Just try and stop me, Darlin," said Liam. "I'm looking forward to visiting you at the estate you were telling me about."

"Oh, and I have so much to show you!" exclaimed Patrice. "The house is even more amazing than I recalled. In fact, I think it was waiting for me."

"Waiting for you?" asked Liam curiously.

"Yes," answered Patrice. "It actually seemed to come to life beginning the very moment I came through the front door."

"Well, there's a big difference between an empty house and one with people living and moving around inside it," said Liam.

"It's more than that," said Patrice. "I think my aunt actually prepared the house to receive me before she passed. Some of the things I've discovered here are truly fascinating."

"I can't wait to see the place." stated Liam. "You've only been there a few days, and I can already feel how excited you are. Just promise me you'll be careful, sweetheart. Old houses have histories, and sometimes the small details we overlook can come back to bite us in the arse."

"I understand that," said Patrice. "And I promise not to over-step my boundaries, I'm just excited because you're coming, and I have so much to share with you."

"I'm counting the minutes myself," said Liam. "Now, I'd better get some rest, because when we start talking shop, we tend to lose all sense of time and I don't want to oversleep and be forced to delay my trip even one moment longer."

"Agreed," said Patrice. "I know you're exhausted, and I promise to take excellent care of you from the moment you arrive, so get some sleep. I don't want you collapsing before you get here."

"Did I tell you that I love you?" asked Liam.

"Almost," replied Patrice.

"I love you very much," said Liam sincerely.

"I love you too, Liam. More than you know." Patrice responded, adding "Goodnight my dear."

"Goodnight, Darlin." replied Liam before reluctantly ending the call. A few seconds later, he was fast asleep.

"He's perfect for you," said Nadine, entering Patrice's study with a cup of hot tea for her. "The perfect counterbalance to your impulsive nature."

"You don't find him boring?" asked Patrice.

"Far from it," Nadine replied. "He's methodical, measured, and extremely intelligent. Just the type of man you need in your life."

"And handsome," said Patrice with a grin.

"Yes, and handsome," agreed Nadine. "Perhaps there's another imaginary friend in our future."

"One step at a time," said Patrice. "First, we need to see how he deals with all of this," she added, gesturing as if to include the entirety of the Lafleur estate.

"Certainly, the true test of a relationship if ever there was one," said Nadine. "But he definitely seems up to the task."

The sound of the telephone ringing on her desk was unexpected and actually startled Patrice for an instant. Both the telephone line and electricity were restored on the same day; however, before now it never rang. Although it was the same number her aunt had for years, it was unlisted, so whoever was calling had either misdialed or they'd gotten the number some other way.

"Hello," said Patrice, answering the phone curiously.

For a moment, there was silence on the other end of the line even though Patrice could hear breathing in the background. It sounded as if someone wanted to speak but didn't quite know what to say. After an elongated pause, the female voice on the other end timidly asked, "May I speak to Naomi Lafleur, please?"

"Unfortunately, Naomi isn't available," said Patrice. "My name is Patrice and I'm her niece. Is there anything I can do for you?"

Another long pause ensued as Patrice waited patiently for the caller to continue. Finally, the woman said, "My mother told me that I needed to speak with Naomi Lafleur, and that she would help me."

"I'm sorry," said Patrice. "My aunt passed away nearly four years ago."

"Oh, no!" said the woman; her voice audibly shaken. A few seconds later, she began to cry.

Responding to the woman's obvious distress, Patrice said "I would be happy to help you if I can... the same way Naomi would have helped you."

The woman on the other end of the line seemed to regain a spark of hope, and with a shaky voice, said "No one believes me, but she just won't let go of me." Her voice cracked at the end of the statement and she began sobbing again.

"Who won't let go of you?" Patrice asked.

"My mother," said the woman, continuing to weep.

"Where are the two of you now?" queried Patrice, attempting to get a better sense of what was happening between the woman and her mother.

"I'm parked on the side of the road near your front gate," said the woman. "My mother guided me here, but I'm not sure I can do this."

"Listen, I'll open the gate for you. You two come up to the house, and we'll figure it out together," said Patrice. "It's alright. My aunt would have wanted me to help you."

After another extended pause, the woman said "Okay," before ending the call.

"She's haunted," said Nadine, standing near Patrice as they watched the silver sedan approach through the window of the study. After parking, a young woman wearing jeans and an oversized turtleneck sweater got out of the car. Her shoulders were sagging, and her eyes barely left the ground as she approached the steps leading up to the house.

Patrice met her at the front door, extending her hand and saying "Hello. I'm Patrice."

"Charlene," said the woman, accepting and weakly shaking Patrice's hand.

"Come in," said Patrice, gesturing toward the study with her right hand while gently placing her hand on the woman's back.

When Charlene tried to step across the threshold into the house, something physically grabbed her sweater, forcefully snatching her back outside and dragging her toward the edge of the porch. As she fell backwards, expecting to tumble down the steps, she didn't.

When she opened her eyes, she was leaning back at a 45-degree angle over the edge of the porch. Patrice was inside the front door with her right arm extended, palm facing outward and fingers spread. Her eyes were closed, and as she drew her hand towards her body, Charlene stood upright and floated gently across the porch to the front door. When she was within reach, Patrice extended her left hand, taking Charlene's arm and pulling her inside the house.

Once inside, the tension at the back of Charlene's sweater immediately slackened, and she fell into Patrice's arms as the door closed behind her. Her eyes wide with astonishment, she stared blankly at the woman holding onto her.

"Welcome to the Lafleur estate," said Patrice with a smile. "Let's try this again, shall we?"

Gently guiding the speechless young woman into her study, Patrice ushered her to a seat at the small table in the center of the room.

Still trying to comprehend what had just happened, Charlene uttered "How did you...?"

"Parlor trick I learned in New Orleans," said Patrice, gesturing as if to dismiss the entire matter as an illusion. "So..." she continued. "Obviously, you're dealing with someone who has separation issues."

"To put it mildly," said Charlene, actually managing a chuckle as she spoke. "My mom passed over a year ago, and since that time, she just refuses to let me move on. I can't even grieve, because..."

The woman's voice cracked again as she buried her face into the sleeves of the sweater covering her hands.

"She doesn't know," said Nadine. "You need to tell her."

Looking at Charlene, Patrice said "I need to tell you something."

"What... what do you mean?" Charlene stammered.

Taking the girls hands in hers—speaking slowly and clearly, Patrice said "The spirit holding onto you is not your mother." after a pause, she added "It's your uncle, Rayland."

Charlene's face went ashen. Her vision blurred completely as her eyes filled with tears that overflowed and ran down her cheeks. "Ray... Ray... Rayland?" she stammered. Her lips were trembling, and her hands were shaking, but she couldn't seem to utter another word.

"He started raping her when she was twelve years old," said Nadine. "He didn't stop until she was seventeen. She ran away from home to get away from him, so he started raping another young girl. He died in prison for that one. His cellmate killed him because he was a pedophile," added Nadine.

"I know what he did, Charlene," said Patrice. "How he hurt you and the others."

"Her mother helped her find you," said Nadine. "She was trying to protect Charlene, but the evil in his spirit was too powerful for her."

"Your mother loves you, Charlene," Patrice said. "She wasn't the one hurting you. She was trying to protect you. That's why she guided you here."

"But I could feel her arms around me in bed at night. She... Oh my god!" cried Charlene. "That was..."

"Yes," interrupted Patrice. "But that stops today."

"But how?" asked Charlene. "As soon as I step outside, he'll be all over me again! I've had nightmares half of my life because of him, and now I find out that even death can't keep him away from me. What am I supposed to do?" she pleaded.

"Nothing," said Patrice. "You go home and rest. Rayland is staying here with me."

Confused, Charlene said "But, how do you know..."

"Trust me," interrupted Patrice. "Rayland will never leave this place again... Ever."

Patrice stood, taking Charlene's hands in hers. "Go in peace. It's alright" she said.

After walking with Patrice to the front door, Charlene hesitated at the threshold.

"Go," said Patrice, with a smile.

When Charlene stepped through the door, it was as if she'd reached oxygen after swimming up from the bottom of the ocean. Her stooped, defeated posture was gone and for the first time in years, she seemed unburdened. At her car, she opened the door and looked back at Patrice, saying "Thank you," before getting inside. A few seconds later, she was driving back down the driveway, through the front gate, and onto the main road.

Patrice watched as the car disappeared down the lane before going back inside the house. In the foyer, Nadine was holding the black specter of Rayland's spirit by what would have passed as the head of a person in human form. She'd snatched him up before he could escape back down the steps into the yard and pulled him inside, closing the door behind him. He was immobilized by the energy sphere surrounding Nadine, but the insults spewing forth from his foul essence were evil and profane. The smell emanating from him was like a mixture of sulfur and skunk urine.

"There were scores of them," said Nadine. "He's been molesting children since he was a teenager, two centuries ago."

Nadine followed Patrice as she climbed the stairs to the second floor. The entity trapped inside her energy sphere was vehemently resisting as Patrice opened the heavy iron door with merely a gesture. The portal in the middle of the room was already glowing as if it were expecting them, and when they approached, the dark chasm at the center opened like the dislocated jaws of an anaconda.

The entity continued to struggle, but the battle was already over for him. With a slight flip of her wrist, Patrice ripped the entity from the comparative comfort of Nadine's energy sphere, crushing it under the enormous pressure of her own. Holding it in front of the portal, it slowly dissolved into a trillion pieces of micro-dust as it was sucked into the black void beyond the gateway. Seconds later, the gateway closed, and the portal vanished without a trace.

The stench which accompanied the malevolent spirit dissipated like tendrils of smoke on a breezy day, and the feelings of balance and levity inside the house quickly returned.

"Well Nadine," said Patrice. "It looks like were open for business."

"One down, thousands to go," said Nadine. "Welcome home, Miss Patrice."

CHAPTER 7

Closing the gateway inside the portal quashed the internal insurrection of malevolent spirits; however, for the multitude of disembodied entities outside it, sensing it re-opening, then closing again was like lighting the lanterns of a coastal lighthouse. Within hours of Charlene's departure, Patrice could feel the energy swell, surrounding the entire property. The portal attracted spirits like moths to a blue flame, and the drip that attracted Charlene would soon be a constant stream.

The house was enormous with eight individual bedrooms. There were two large suites on the ground floor, four large bedrooms on the second floor, and two more at opposite ends of the third floor beneath the slanted rafters of the ceiling. As children, Naomi and Juliette occupied the bedrooms on the third floor. They were smaller than the other rooms in the house but allowed the twins to be close to one another without sacrificing the expression of their own individual personalities. Their parents occupied the suite opposite Grandma Marie's sanctuary on the ground floor.

Over the years, the house experienced varying levels of occupancy as generations of Lafleur children were born, grew up, departed, returned, bore new generations of children, grew older, and passed the family torch for nearly four centuries. With Patrice and Nadine being the sole occupants, it felt like a seasonal retreat boarded up for the off season and staffed with only a skeleton crew.

In anticipation of Liam's arrival, Patrice and Nadine prepared the second suite on the first floor. It was a beautiful space, actually larger than Patrice's sanctuary with a fireplace and a large library closed off by glass-paned double French doors. The space was Francois Lafleur's pride and joy, and he'd spared no expense when designing it. After the fire, he expanded it even further, creating a truly luxurious master chamber. In addition to the entrance through the spacious family room, there was a separate exit leading out onto the concrete walkway that wrapped around the house.

Within two weeks of her arrival, she and Nadine had made amazing progress in reclaiming the space on the ground floor. They installed rows of shelves in two of the three open bedrooms on the second floor and moved all the accumulated relics into them. Patrice's background in anthropology and archeology proved quite useful in sorting the objects into specific categories and creating a database that allowed for their quick location and retrieval. The third bedroom on the second floor was converted into a storeroom, and all of the unused furniture from the other rooms was placed inside it for safekeeping.

By the day Liam arrived, Patrice had replaced all of the old furniture in the master chamber except for the things inside the Library, which she decided to leave unaltered. It gave the room a sense of historic elegance that made her feel connected to her ancestors. Besides, she couldn't bear the thought of parting with the ornate, hand-crafted desk and matching armchair placed there by Francois Lafleur himself. Once completed, the suite was modern and elegant, with just the right number of antique accents to tie the room together with the rest of the house.

When Patrice met Liam at the curbside pickup area of the small regional airport in Shreveport, she was bubbling with excitement. The bearded giant of a man, seemed completely out of place yet warmly familiar to her as she sprang out of the vehicle and ran up to him, leaping into his arms. They encircled her immediately and he hugged her body close to him as their lips found each other's.

After a kiss long enough to make everyone around them *extremely uncomfortable*, he lowered her to the ground, piercing her soul and melting her heart all over again with those mesmerizing green eyes and perfect smile. "You're getting skinny, lassie!" Liam said. "Don't they make a proper stew here in Louisiana?"

Smiling like a teenage schoolgirl, Patrice said "I'm already hanging around your neck, so you don't have to flatter me anymore."

"Seriously!" said Liam. "I nearly snapped you in half, Darlin!"

"Well, that's because you're such a big strong man, Liam," Patrice replied, playfully batting her eyes.

Laughing, he kissed her again before saying, "Honestly, you look fantastic, Patrice. You're positively glowing."

"That's because of you, sweetheart," Patrice replied. "I am so happy you're here. I've missed you so much."

"I've missed you too, Darlin," said Liam. "And I'm so happy to finally be here with you."

After loading his bags into the back of her SUV, they left the airport. Within half an hour, the sun had set, and they were pulling up to, and through the gate at the Lafleur estate. As it closed behind them and they approached the house, Liam's jaw dropped, and his eyes widened in amazement.

"Christ Almighty!" he exclaimed. "There are castles in Scotland that are smaller than this place!"

"Wait until you see the inside," Patrice replied. "It's dark right now, but tomorrow morning I'll give you the grand tour."

They were barely inside the house before Patrice grabbed his hand, leading him through the sprawling family room and towards the newly renovated bedroom suite. As they made their way through the house, Liam's eyes were darting about as if he were exploring the National Museum in Edinburgh.

Dragging him into the bedroom, Patrice closed the doors behind them; slowly backing him towards the yet-to-be-christened king-size bed. With a trail of discarded clothing littering the floor behind her, she said, "The grand tour can wait until morning. I have another deep exploration project that requires your immediate attention tonight."

Fourteen days had been an eternity for them, and they were both anxious to make up for lost time. As their passions collided, their union was reenacted several times during the night before the North American Nightingales surrendered the stage to the Louisiana Waterthrushes and the grey morning sky.

After nearly two solid days of air travel and a night of blissful lovemaking, Liam was exhausted and slept until nearly 10:00 a.m. before the smell of breakfast gently tugged him from his extended slumber. When he sat up in bed, Patrice was just entering the room with a tray of bacon and eggs, fresh fruit, black coffee, and toasted English muffins.

Smiling at Patrice, he said "I'm sorry Miss, but I didn't realize I'd checked into the Waldorf Astoria."

"Nothing but the best for guests of the Lafleur Estate," said Patrice, taking a seat on the bed beside him. After kissing him good morning, she said "I trust you slept well."

"For some reason, I was tossing and turning all night," Liam said with a sly smile.

"Yeah. Tossing me onto my back, and turning me on all night," quipped Patrice playfully.

"Is *that* what it was?" replied Liam. "Well thanks for clearing that up for me," he added with a smile, before digging into the hearty meal Patrice had prepared for him.

After breakfast, Liam put on his slacks and shirt, and Patrice led him out of the bedroom to show him the rest of the house. As they wandered around the ground floor, he was fascinated by the architecture. While the exterior of the plantation style manor could have been expected, the interior design cues were unmistakably seventeenth century French, and it was obvious the estate was built for European aristocrats.

As they progressed up the curved staircase, Liam was seriously impressed by the attention to detail and fine craftsmanship that went into nearly every element of the house. "This is incredible," he said. "It's like the house was built only a year or two ago. The wood seams are so precisely fitted and aligned, and there isn't a buckled plank or warped floorboard in the entire house. In this climate, that is almost certainly an impossibility."

"There are a lot of things about this house that would seem to be certain impossibilities," Patrice replied, leading the way into the first of the rooms housing the collection of relics and artifacts. Liam's eyes were as wide as saucers as he bounded indiscriminately from rack to rack, inspecting and marveling at the assortment of rarities populating the shelves. Unlike Patrice, he actually knew the origins of most of the items; even those that were so rare, they were assumed to be myths and urban legends.

Time after time, he would freeze in his tracks, awestruck by yet another relic thought to have been lost to history forever, yet there they were, safe and sound within the racks of the Lafleur estate.

After several hours spent inside the first of the two large rooms on the second floor, Patrice suggested they take a break to have a late-afternoon snack in the kitchen. Nadine had already prepared something for them and left the room as Patrice entered with Liam. While they ate, Liam's mind was reeling as he considered the historical value of so many items hidden away in only *one* of the rooms upstairs. They'd spent hours there already and hadn't even come close to examining everything. He could only imagine what they would discover once they began exploring the second room.

"Have you any idea how valuable some of the things upstairs would be to a museum or avid collector?" asked Liam. "You could literally make up ridiculous numbers for dozens of items up there, and curators would break their necks trampling over one another to be the first in line to pay for it! There are literally world-renowned academic scholars and archeologists scouring the deserts of Egypt, Saudi Arabia, Syria, and Jordan, looking for the Eye of Idris, and your aunt had it here in this house the entire time!"

Patrice smiled at Nadine, standing in the hallway outside the kitchen, as Liam gesticulated wildly while describing article after article and the sheer incredulity of their existence, let alone the fact that it's just sitting there on the shelf in a room in a house in a place like Shreveport. Nadine obviously liked Liam. The same traits that appealed to Patrice, struck a natural chord with Nadine because she was the manifested essence of Patrice's own character, but without the need to rationalize away the flaws that love tends to obscure. As a result, she was more objective in her views, and she deeply approved of Liam.

After their late lunch, Patrice and Liam headed for the stairs to continue their tour. At the steps, Liam paused to ask, "How late does your assistant work? I was rambling on so much, I nearly overlooked her, and I certainly don't want to appear rude."

Patrice froze in her tracks! Suddenly, it was her turn to be at a complete and utter loss for words. "What did you say?" she asked, clearly taken aback by Liam's simple question.

"The young woman in the hallway," said Liam. "How late does she work?"

For over thirty years, Nadine had been an extension of Patrice, even considering the twenty-year hiatus. In all that time, no one—not even Naomi—had ever been able to see her. Now, Liam stood next to her, casually asking about Nadine as if it were the most normal thing in the world.

"Patrice," said Liam, hesitantly. "Is something wrong?"

"You can see her?" asked Patrice, obviously shocked. "You can actually see Nadine?"

"Why wouldn't I be able to see her?" asked Liam. "She's standing right there in the kitchen doorway," he added.

"Liam, Honey," said Patrice, her eyes now wide in amazement. "I am the *only* person who has ever seen her. She's been a part of me since I was a child, but everyone called her my imaginary friend, because none of them could really see her."

"Well, as sure as I'm standing her talking to you, I can see her standing right over..."

When he looked toward the kitchen doorway, Nadine was gone. Quickly turning back to face Patrice again, he discovered Nadine was suddenly standing there, right beside her.

"How on earth...?" said Liam, surprised but in no way shaken. "She was just over..."

"She's my spiritual channel," interrupted Patrice. "When I was a little girl, I was the only child within a mile of the estate. There was no one I could talk to, or play with, or share my secrets with, so I asked Aunt Naomi if I could use one of the ledgers in her office to start a diary. I didn't realize it at the time, but it was really an enchanted grimoire, and when I named the diary Nadine, she appeared two days later, and has been here in the house ever since."

"Your channel?" queried Liam. "You mean like a crystal ball or an enchanted mirror or something?"

"Actually, she's exactly like that," agreed Patrice. "As far as I know, Nadine is the first spiritual channel to have ever been manifested as a physical entity. When I was a child, she was a child. When I came back as an adult, she changed, becoming a more accurate reflection of who *I've* become."

"And she can just materialize out of thin air?" asked Liam. "Just like that?"

"Not out of thin air," said Patrice. "She is a spiritual extension of me, but she can accomplish things I need done independently, without me having to be in the same room with her. Her only limitation is that her field of influence is limited to the house, and a few yards in each direction beyond the walls of the building."

"Fascinating," said Liam, reaching out and attempting to touch her arm. His fingertips passed right through her as if she were a hologram; however, visually she seemed just as real as Patrice, who was standing right next to her.

"For an apparition to form this clearly, especially in a sunlit area like this, it would require an incredibly powerful energy source to tap into," stated Liam. "In order for her to physically manipulate objects, that source would need to be constant and stable. Where in the world is, she getting it from?"

"The house *is* the source," said Patrice. "It's surrounded by an energy field that both protects it, and allows me and Nadine to use that energy to help others, just as it did for my aunt Naomi and my grandmother Marie, and her mother, and her mother, and so on, dating back to the mid-1600s when Marguerite Lafleur discovered it."

"You told me about your family and their history as spiritual healers and such, but you never mentioned Nadine before," said Liam.

"Because, I didn't remember her," said Patrice. "My memories of her were suppressed by my aunt Naomi when I departed for college. She didn't want me using either the knowledge of Nadine or my other gifts for personal gain or to advance my own self-interests."

"Karmic backlash," said Liam, nodding understandably. "She was protecting you."

"Yes," said Patrice, slightly tilting her head and smiling at Liam's awareness of such a thing. "I'm impressed!" she added, nodding her head in approval.

"That explains a lot," said Liam. "The sheer number of rare and ancient artifacts that found their way into this house should have been a dead give-away. I'm surprised I didn't recognize it sooner."

"What do you mean?" asked Patrice curiously.

"Artifacts and relics like the ones accumulated here, are drawn to energy sources like this house, because of its proximity to spiritual gateways," Liam explained. "They are mostly protective talismans that serve to prevent the proliferation of evil spirits that could emerge from them. In order to attract the sheer number of artifacts you have here, there must be an immense energy portal either inside the house, or in close proximity to it. That's why this house is in such immaculate structural shape. The energy from such a portal is like armor plating for a battleship. It can literally prevent structures from aging for hundreds, if not thousands of years, and with the presence of so many powerful protective artifacts bolstering the house's sphere of protection, the evil which could emerge from such a gateway must be unfathomable; thus, the overwhelming presence of additional protective measures."

Staring at Liam as if he'd just hung the moon and stars, Patrice said "Liam, you are a brilliant, brilliant man." Stepping closer and putting her arms around him, she said "I've been asking myself how to break the news and explain all of this stuff to you, and you zip through all of my doubts and worries in minutes... just like you've always done."

"Patrice, you've entrusted me with knowledge of the most significant archeological find, possibly in the history of the world!" said Liam, hugging her tightly. "You cannot begin to imagine how much that means to me!"

Pulling his face to hers, Patrice kissed him deeply from her very soul. Ending the kiss and pulling away after a long moment, she took his hand saying, "Come with me. I've got one more thing to show you."

Leading him up the stairs to the second floor, this time she led him down the long corridor to the right. As they stood there facing what appeared for Liam to be a solid iron wall, Patrice raised her right hand and with a slightest of gestures, the massive iron door opened inward. Inside the room, the portal was glowing, but the gateway remained tightly shut.

"Oh my god!" said Liam slowly. "It's incredible!"

"This is what my ancestors have been protecting for centuries," Patrice explained. "The portal secures a gateway for the banishment of malevolent entities into the nether realms."

Turning to face a visibly stunned Liam, she added, "And I am its Guardian."

CHAPTER 8

"I let you out of my sight for two weeks, and when I see you again, you live in an enchanted castle with a ghost, and more priceless artifacts than the London Museum," said Liam with a smile.

"Don't forget I'm the guardian of the portal," added Patrice, nodding to herself while staring blankly across the room.

"Oh yes," said Liam. "We certainly don't want to overlook *that* little nuance."

Sitting on the loveseat in the family room outside the master chamber, Liam and Patrice seemed as if they'd been living there together for years. Despite the events of just the past forty-eight hours, neither of them seemed particularly concerned or distracted.

In Jordan, they had made it a habit to decompress after work by leaving the dig site and finding a place where they could look up into the stars and reflect on the accomplishments of the day. While the number of revelations here was unheard of, the process and the purpose were exactly the same. When researchers are too closely focused on the objects discovered they can easily miss the larger picture. If ever there was a larger picture to be considered, it was here at the Lafleur estate.

There were mystical objects here from every continent on the planet. The odds of so many of them showing up in one place, *anywhere* on Earth were incalculable, regardless of the location. Nevertheless, upstairs in this house were protective amulets, scrolls, talismans, and charms of all shapes and sizes. The real question here was, "Why?"

The possibility of it all being attributed to coincidence could clearly be dismissed out of hand. Liam's analytical methodology could boil nearly any body of evidence down to a single motive or purpose given time—the key factor being time. In this case, there were too many objects in one place for their *origins* to be the key.

"We need to stop thinking about where all of the artifacts came from," said Liam. "At this point, it really doesn't matter anymore because they are all right here."

"Yes," answered Patrice. "And my aunt was abundantly clear about the value of the items being karmically connected to the accuracy of her Tarot readings. That's why she never even attempted to have them appraised. She simply accepted them and stored them until their purpose revealed itself.

As a kid, I always assumed that by 'value', she meant the amount of money she could get for them, but now when I think about it, she had enough customers who paid in cash to cover the cost of maintaining the estate."

"Your aunt was a very wise and powerful guardian," said Liam. "She almost certainly knew why these items were showing up on her doorstep in such a steady stream." Looking to Patrice, he asked "Did your aunt ever speak to you or anyone else about the artifacts she assembled here?"

Suddenly, Patrice's eyes widened. "Elenore!" she said excitedly.

"Elenore?" Liam asked.

"Yes," Patrice replied. "Elenore knows everything about anything that's ever happened here. I'm sure she can shed some light on the subject."

"I'd assume you're not talking about a three-hundred-year-old woman, but I don't think it's safe to assume anything regarding this place."

"Three-hundred-seventy-five, but who's counting?" said Patrice. Noticing Liam's puzzled expression, she clarified "Elenore was the original grimoire started by Marguerite Lafleur when she discovered the portal back in 1642. Since that time, the records of every guardian in my family's history has been included in that ledger, and I'm betting something like that wouldn't have escaped their attention."

"Can we..." started Liam, before being cut off in mid-sentence.

"No," interrupted Patrice. "*We* can't, but I can."

Continuing, she said "The one place in the entire house I cannot allow you to enter, is the sanctuary containing the grimoire. It's sealed to anyone other than the current portal guardian, and the grimoire itself cannot be removed from there."

"I suppose I could write down some of the questions we'll need answers for, but it's tough to know what to ask without knowing where the information will lead, and which follow-up questions will arise," said Liam.

"That could take hours or even days without you being able to actually read the journal," said Patrice. "But like I said before. You can't go in there, and the journal cannot leave the sanctuary."

"It doesn't need to," said Nadine, who was now mysteriously standing in the doorway of the family room.

Liam and Patrice were suddenly all ears. Liam, because Nadine had magically appeared out of nowhere, and Patrice, because she was anxious to hear Nadine's proposal.

Approaching the two of them, Nadine said "Your aunt said to treat the journal as a living thing, and the knowledge you seek will always be revealed to you. Well, I am now part of that journal, and since Liam has no problem seeing and communicating with me, perhaps we should all just have a conversation."

For a moment, Patrice and Liam just sat there, staring first at each other, then back towards Nadine, and then at each other again. Finally, as if anticipating the question from Liam as to why she hadn't thought of that earlier, Patrice said "Don't look at me. Three days ago, she was a little girl!"

"True," said Liam. "That would've been a pretty steep learning curve, considering everything else going on around here." After a brief pause, he said "How about we table that discussion for in the morning? Right now, I'd like to enjoy an evening outside the castle and I'm sure there's an Irish pub here somewhere."

"You know," said Patrice. "That's a great idea. I've only been outside the gate twice since I got here, and I could use a little time away from this place, although I'm not sure we'll be able to find an Irish pub."

"If you put three Irishman in a town, one of them will open a pub so the other two have a place to fight." said Liam, almost too casually. "And believe me... Every cabbie knows where it is."

Sure enough, half an hour later their UBER driver was dropping them off at Fatty Arbuckle's Pub near the Red River. It was only a little over a mile from the estate and was actually quite authentic, serving a broad selection of ales, and a fairly decent Irish stew to boot. Liam and Patrice took a booth near the back of the pub where they ate, drank, and talked for hours. Before they knew it, midnight was upon them, and with the size of the task ahead of them, they decided to text their UBER driver to pick them up.

The driver replied, letting them know he'd be there in ten minutes or so. One hour later, he still hadn't arrived. When Patrice texted him again, he didn't reply, and when she called, he didn't answer. While it was odd, they didn't harp on it, and simply asked the barkeep to call them a cab. The cab driver arrived only a couple of minutes later and called the pub to let them know he was outside.

They settled the tab with the barkeep before exiting the pub, and when Liam opened the car door for Patrice at the curb, the smell coming from inside the vehicle was wretched. When the driver turned and looked toward the back seat, his features were horribly distorted by the entity encasing him like thick black tar. Backing away from the car, Patrice put her left hand over her mouth and nose, trying not to vomit on the sidewalk.

Liam couldn't see or smell anything, and for a moment he thought she might be staggering drunk. Before he could say a word, Patrice raised her right hand, pushing the door handle from Liam's grip and shoving the whole vehicle ten feet sideways, away from the curb and the two of them.

Stunned, Liam ask "What the hell is going on?"

"It's the cab driver," said Patrice. "He's possessed and completely consumed by evil."

"And you can see that?!" queried Liam, shocked by the unexpected development.

"I can see it, smell it, and feel it!" Patrice replied. "He killed our UBER driver, and had we gotten into that car, he'd have driven it into a bridge abutment or plunged it right into the river."

In the street, the driver's side door opened at the possessed man exited, walking directly toward them. To Liam, he appeared to be normal but the voice coming from him was speaking ancient Gaelic laced with a constant stream of the most obscene profanities Liam had ever heard. As the man quickly rushed towards them, Liam stepped forward leaning into it as his huge fist struck the man's left jawbone. Liam felt the bone break as the blow sent the man tumbling back out into the street. No sooner than he'd stopped rolling on the ground, he rose back to his feet staggering toward them again.

As Liam stepped up to the plate to take another swing, Patrice extended her hand, saying "Liam, No! Don't touch him again!"

The man seemed to have encountered an invisible barrier which prevented him from coming closer. As he struggled against it, Patrice slowly ripped away the dark mass cloaking the man's aura. Once the two were separated, the man fell to the ground while Patrice held the now visible black mass suspended about five feet in the air. Even though it was now completely detached, it continued to struggle as she contained it.

"The portal is too far away!" she exclaimed. "What am I supposed to do with this thing?"

"The river!" said Liam. "You can drown demons in running water, but it needs to remain submerged for several minutes until its malevolent energy is drained and it dies!"

Patrice lifted her hand higher, raising the evil mass into the air as she hurried around the corner of the pub. Once she could see the river, she plunged the demon into the water and held it there. She could feel it struggling, and without the proximity of the portal feeding her own energy, it was a toss-up as to who would run out of steam first.

After picking up the unconscious but breathing cab driver and carrying him out of the street, Liam laid him on the sidewalk before rushing around the building to Patrice. She was struggling with the entity who was desperate to escape death in the black water of the Red River. After several tense minutes, the demon began to weaken, and soon thereafter, the boiling in the river surrounding it calmed and resumed its quiet pace with nary a ripple.

Patrice finally released her grip on the energy field and collapsed into Liam's waiting arms.

When she opened her eyes again, she was in bed inside the master chamber at the estate. Liam was asleep, spooned in with his arms wrapped around her like twin boa constrictors. Her head was pounding; although, she wasn't sure whether it was due to the demonic encounter, or the hours-long quaff session at the pub with Liam.

"How are you feeling?" came Liam's burly Scottish voice from behind her.

"Aside from my head feeling eight times too large and filled with golf balls and Jell-O, things couldn't be better," answered Patrice. "What time is it anyway?" she asked.

"Almost noon, I imagine," Liam replied.

Turning to face him, she asked "What happened to the demon?"

"You got him," said Liam. "The rushing water in the river worked."

"What about the cab driver?" Patrice asked, recalling how she'd separated them.

"I told the barkeep he stumbled and fell against the curb when he came around the car to open the door for us. He called an ambulance, then he and a couple of his customers came out and carried the cabbie inside," said Liam. "He was out cold, and his jaw was broken, but I'm sure he'll be fine.

"How did we get back here?" wondered Patrice. "I can't remember anything after the river."

"Well, I wasn't going to leave you there, and I sure as hell wasn't calling another taxi!" said Liam. "It was only a mile or so, so I carried you."

"You *carried* me?!" asked Patrice, astounded. "A mile?" she added.

"Or so," said Liam. "'T'was a lovely night for a stroll anyway."

Of the myriad of words vying for pole position in her mind at that moment, the two that crossed the finish line were "Thank you," uttered almost as a whisper before she kissed him and hugged herself close to him again.

"For you the world, Darlin," said Liam. "But we have a whole new basket of cats to corral now."

"What do you mean?" asked Patrice.

"You leave the estate for dinner and a pint or two, and a demon tries to kidnap you," said Liam. "Something big is brewing here, and we don't even know the half of it."

"I was afraid you were going to say that," said Patrice. "It's not like I didn't see it, but hearing you say it out loud, makes it real now." There were tears in her eyes when she looked at him, saying "I can't put you in that kind of danger, Liam. As long as you're here with me, they'll come after you too, and I would die if anything happened to you."

"Well, you can't face a problem and solve it until you're able to admit that it's actually a problem," said Liam. "We have everything we need to find a solution, right here in this house, and I'm not going anywhere until we do." After kissing her forehead, he added, "I didn't fly halfway around the world to get to you, just to be scared off by some zombie cab driver. Besides, judging by the way things are escalating despite all of the protective artifacts amassed here, I don't believe there will be a safe place for anyone on Earth, unless we can figure out what's happening before it boils over."

"I love you Liam," said Patrice. "And if anyone can make sense of this mess, I know it's got to be you."

"We're stronger together," said Liam. "Now; I'd suggest we drag ourselves out of bed and make a strong pot of coffee. I think it's high time we sat down with Nadine to have that conversation."

CHAPTER 9

As the three of them sat in the study, Patrice sat behind her desk while Liam and Nadine sat across from her. Liam was still astounded at Nadine's density as a non-corporeal entity, but the mere point that he could see her seemed as matter of fact with him as it had been with Patrice after her first night in the estate. Clearly, Liam's connection to Patrice and his unquestionable belief in her abilities, made the presence of Nadine an uncontested truth in his mind.

The conversation began with Patrice asking Nadine, "Has Elenore foretold of anything which could explain the sudden increase in the malevolent energy we are now experiencing?"

"There is no specific reference to this sort of event, but the increase in the energy levels of dark entities was predictable with the extended absence of a portal guardian," answered Nadine. "Once you arrived, their influence immediately began to evaporate because it was counteracted by your energy."

"What about all of the protective artifacts assembled here?" asked Liam. "Are there any commonalities between them which could shed light on what might be headed our way?"

"According to Elenore, each of them was created to shield against evil entities specific to the spiritual cultures and traditions of their own civilizations," said Nadine. "There is no commonality between those specific entities identified within the journal."

"Perhaps we need to be less specific and more general," noted Patrice. "Just because the names of the entities differ, doesn't mean their intentions do."

"Exactly," noted Liam, asking "Without regard to the specific entities for which each talisman was created to protect against, is there any relationship between the threat those entities posed to the civilizations who created them?"

After a long pause in which Nadine seemed to be scanning an occult database, she answered "There are four that ward off demons who eat children, five of them prevent famine created by malevolent demi-gods, seven are meant to bind entities who sow mischief, ten of them shield against plagues in various forms, fourteen prevent infertility, fifty-eight of them drain the energy of poltergeists, seventy…"

"Hold on," said Liam. "is there any one specific purpose that either all or most of them share, regardless to what degree?"

After another pause, Nadine said "There are four-thousand-twenty-two artifacts assembled here, of which four-thousand-eighteen are meant to set physical borders against the incursion of powerful malevolent spirits; however, the entities they were created to repel are all different."

"Do you mean the entities are different, or the *names* of the entities are different?" asked Liam.

"There is not enough information here to make that determination," said Nadine. "Elenore's cultural base was created from French, English, European, and American cultures, so the list of names for the specific entities is largely incomplete."

"The journal was created and maintained by my ancestors who lived in this house dating back to the 1600s," said Patrice. "Although; the people we've helped over the centuries would certainly have come from cultures and backgrounds scattered around the entire world."

"True," said Liam. "For the most part, people don't even know why their families hung onto these things over the years, and by the time they come across them, the person who originally acquired them is long gone."

"So," said Patrice. "How many of those four thousand plus objects do not have any occult protective properties, or act to repel anything? Perhaps they can do something we've been overlooking."

"There are only two items which have no protective qualities at all, but both would certainly be considered priceless artifacts despite that fact," said Nadine. "One is the Staff of Osiris, and the other is..."

"The Eye of Idris!" exclaimed Liam, cutting off Nadine in mid-sentence while springing to his feet-- flailing about excitedly and dancing around the study.

"Yes," replied Nadine, curiously watching Liam's victory dance.

Patrice looked completely lost in the exchange. Her eyes darting back and forth between Nadine and Liam, she asked "Okay, what am I missing here?"

"My dear!" exclaimed Liam "You aren't missing anything! In fact, you have it all!"

After waiting and allowing Liam a moment to gather his thoughts and settle down again, Patrice asked "Would you like to fill in the blanks here, or are you going to just let me squirm?"

Leaning on the right side of Patrice's desk, Liam smiled back and forth between Patrice and Nadine before saying, "According to legend, Idris and Osiris are the same person! Idris was born in Babylon but died in Egypt. Some people believe Idris to have been buried in one of the two largest pyramids on the Giza plateau near Cairo."

"Focus, Liam," said Patrice. "We'll do the history lesson afterwards, but the suspense is killing me!"

Looking at Patrice, Liam said "Idris *is* Osiris!" After a pause, he said "The Staff of Osiris, was created to hold the Eye of Idris!"

Noting Patrice had not yet made the connection, Liam said "The Eye was created in Iraq where Idris was born, but the Staff was made in Egypt where he died. Both the Staff and the Eye belonged to Idris, who the Egyptians knew as Osiris!"

As the realization dawned on Patrice, her eyes grew wide with excitement! "You're saying, we have both the Eye of Idris and the Staff of Osiris, and somehow they were both designed to fit together for some reason!"

"Yes!" exclaimed Liam. "The Eye of Idris was an amplifier capable of creating unheard of energy levels by focusing the power of other artifacts like a prism. However, whoever was holding the Eye would have been instantly consumed by the heat generated while focusing such an enormous energy burst. The Staff was over two meters long, but with Osiris being a giant standing nearly five meters tall, the depictions of the staff in Egyptian hieroglyphics are misleading. The staff allowed Idris, or Osiris, to hold the Eye above his head while isolating him from the heat created when a focused beam of energy was discharged."

"I remember the staff from my first day going through everything," said Patrice. "I thought it was a shepherd's hook."

"A common misconception," said Liam. "However, the outer edge of the Eye of Idris is grooved. The loop at the top of the Staff flexes open just enough for the Eye to snap firmly into place. There are countless Egyptian hieroglyphics depicting the Staff of Osiris, and a few which actually depict the Eye of Idris inside the staff; however, most scholars fail to notice the subtle differences in depictions where the Eye is inserted, and where it's not."

Purely out of curiosity, Patrice pulled up several images of Osiris using an internet search and was surprised to see Liam was correct. In most of the images, the hooked staff of Osiris was empty; however, in a few of the images, it was now painfully clear that the hook at the top of the staff was most definitely holding the Eye of Idris. In fact, one image she discovered showed Osiris holding the staff without the eye, while over his left shoulder behind him, the eye is shown inside the staff.

"Oh my god!" exclaimed Patrice. I've been looking at pictures of Osiris now for over twenty years, and I have never even noticed this before!"

"It's very subtle, and many a skilled eye has missed it, attributing the difference to the background coloring or the lack thereof, in the hieroglyphics," explained Liam. "But now, all of the speculation goes right out the window, because you have both of them here in this house!"

Suddenly, there was an unspoken urgency for Liam and Patrice to rush up the stairs to the second floor. Having had no idea, the two items were related, Patrice had placed the Eye of Idris on a rack with other glass, crystal, and gem-type artifacts. The Staff of Osiris was in the second room on a rack with other staffs, canes, and wooden tools and instruments. Upon discovering both items where Patrice had placed them, the temptation to insert the Eye into the Staff was nearly overwhelming. Nevertheless, Liam let caution override curiosity until they could more accurately gauge the possible repercussions of such and act.

"Before we do anything, we need to make sure we're not creating an event we cannot control," said Liam. "Supposedly, this instrument could generate an energy beam powerful enough to reach beyond the outer edge of our solar system. I'll need to do a lot more research before I'm comfortable uniting these two artifacts."

"I agree," said Patrice. "We certainly don't want to create the apocalypse we're trying to prevent."

"Nadine," asked Liam "How long have these two artifacts been here at the estate?"

"The Staff arrived in the year 1702, and the Eye in 1985," said Nadine.

"Wow!" said Liam. "I didn't think they'd be separated by that many years."

"Neither did I," said Patrice. "Perhaps they don't have anything to do with whatever is coming."

"For nearly everything else in this house, I might be inclined to believe that, but for these two items, that would be like striking the same gnat twice with two different bar darts," said Liam. "Besides, having them here in this house means nothing if those living here are unable to see the connection between them."

"In other words," said Patrice. "The fact that these items are here, is less important than *us* being here at this particular moment in time to recognize their significance."

"That's the vibe I'm getting," said Liam. "They arrived almost three hundred years apart from one another, but we arrived within two weeks of each other. That's got to mean something."

"I'm with you on that," said Patrice. "I suggest that you and I do what we do best; start digging and looking for answers. If there's a connection, we *will* find it."

Leaving the artifacts where Patrice and Nadine had placed them, Patrice and Liam reconvened in the study, wordlessly diving into their research. Between the two of them, they had hundreds of exclusive information resources they could tap for answers, and they would leave no stone unturned.

They'd been working non-stop for hours when the intercom at the front gate buzzed, snatching them back to reality. Pressing the TALK button on the receiver in her study, Patrice said "Can I help you?"

"I hope so," said the voice on the other end. "I'm Detective Broussard from the Shreveport Police Department. I'm here with Detective Tate, and we're investigating an incident regarding an UBER driver yesterday evening. I was wondering if we might be able to have a word with you?"

"Of course," said Patrice, looking at Liam with a raised eyebrow. "I'll buzz you in."

"They're legitimate," said Nadine. "There's no supernatural contamination in their auras, but their auras are dark. They are very disturbed by what they are investigating."

"Thank you," said Patrice as Nadine vanished into the woodwork. "Wait here," she said to Liam before walking to the front door to meet the two detectives.

Nadine was correct in analyzing the detective's auras. They were dark and troubled as the two men exited their vehicle and walked up the steps to the front door.

"Good evening, Miss Lafleur," said the lead detective. "I'm Detective Broussard and this is Detective Tate."

Still at the doorway, Patrice asked "What can I do for you, Detectives?"

"Would you mind if we come inside?" asked Detective Broussard. "It's been a long day, and we're nearly dead on our feet."

"Of course," said Patrice. "Please. Come in."

Leading them into the study, she said "This is Professor Liam McKenna from the University of Glasgow in Scotland," as Liam stood up extending his arm to shake both their hands in turn.

"Good evening, Professor," said Detective Broussard. "What brings you all the way to Shreveport?" he asked with a forced smile.

"She let you in the front door," said Liam, nodding toward Patrice.

"I can certainly understand that." said the Detective. "I hope you're able to enjoy our little town during your stay."

"Thank you," said Liam, moving over to stand beside Patrice.

"Please have a seat Detectives," said Patrice. "Can I offer you something to drink? Coffee, tea, water or soft drinks or anything?"

"No Ma'am but thank you for the hospitality," said Detective Broussard. "We're investigating an accident reported late last night and hoping you could shed some light on a few things for us."

"What sort of accident?" asked Patrice.

"The UBER driver that picked you up here yesterday evening was involved in a fatal accident a little after midnight, and we're trying to reconstruct the timeline of the accident," said the detective.

"Oh my god!" said Patrice. "I texted him to pick us up, but he never showed. We had no idea he was in an accident!"

"What time was that text sent?" asked the detective. "Do you happen to recall?"

"As a matter of fact, it should still be in my text messages," said Patrice while retrieving her mobile phone from the desk drawer. Pulling up the message, she said "It was sent at 12:07 a.m. according to my SMS text log. He responded one minute later, saying he'd be there soon to pick us up."

"So, he responded at 12:08, and how long did he say it would take for him to get there?" asked the detective.

"According to his text, he said about ten minutes," answered Patrice. "We waited an hour, and when he didn't show up, I texted him again. He didn't reply so I called him, but he didn't answer."

"Yes Ma'am," said the detective. "That seems to match what his phone log says." Looking at Patrice and Liam, he asked "Did he seem upset, or depressed when he picked you up? Was there anything unusual in his behavior towards either of you?"

"Quite the opposite," said Patrice. "In fact, he was right on time, he greeted us with a smile, and was extremely courteous. We gave him a big tip, so he'd be available to pick us up when we were ready to leave."

"So, nothing unusual. No complaints about his day or anything?" asked Detective Broussard.

"No," said Patrice. "He was a model driver. We couldn't have been more pleased with him." Curiously, she asked "What happened? Was this more than just a traffic accident?"

Looking quickly to Detective Tate, then back to Patrice, Detective Broussard said "It just seems odd he would drop you off, get a big tip, pick up and drop off three more fares, respond to your text telling you he'd be there in ten minutes, then peel out of the gas station parking lot and cross into oncoming traffic to collide head-on with a cement truck, only one minute after responding to your text."

"Oh my god!" exclaimed Patrice. "That's horrible!"

"Somehow, it seems a lot of horrible things happen when it comes to this house, Miss Lafleur."

"What are you saying," asked Patrice. "Do you think that I had something to do with this?" she added, shocked at the insinuation.

"Are you gentlemen accusing Miss Lafleur of something, or just letting your own fears and superstitions cause you to make unfounded assertions?" asked Liam, visibly irritated.

"What about the taxi driver who came to pick you up when your UBER driver didn't show?" asked the detective. "Somehow, he ended up in the hospital with a broken jaw and his entire body covered in some sort of occult markings cut into his flesh." Peering at Patrice over the top of his eyeglasses, he added "Wasn't your aunt a witch, and your mother, a drug addict and a whore?"

All the moisture inside Patrice's mouth dried up, and her eyesight narrowed into what seemed a dark tunnel to her. The room was spinning, and she thought she was about to pass out.

"I think it's time for you gentlemen to leave!" said Liam, stepping between Detective Broussard and Patrice.

"Okay, okay… We're leaving," said the detective, throwing up his hands before walking through the study back towards the front door.

Liam escorted them out of the house and onto the porch as Patrice stood in the study, speechless with tears of rage streaming down her face.

"The next time you show up here, you'd better have a warrant! Otherwise, you two assholes can sit in front of the gate and piss down each other's legs!"

The two detectives slowly ambled towards their unmarked cruiser in the driveway. Before getting into the vehicle, Detective Broussard said "Mr. McKenna, are you going to be in town for a few days? We may have more questions for you as our investigation develops."

"If you have any questions, you can contact my attorney," said Liam.

"Yeah, I'm sure you'll have your hands full, banging your witch," said the detective under his breath, but loud enough for Liam to hear as he entered the vehicle on the passenger side.

As Liam leapt off of the porch, sprinting towards the cruiser, the two detectives sped off, kicking dirt and gravel into the air in their wake.

Liam was livid as he stormed back into the house. Patrice was standing in the middle of the study with her fists tightly clenched and tears streaming down her face. Without a word, Liam approached, enveloping her in his powerful embrace, and holding her until the tremors of rage subsided.

"I wanted to kill them," said Patrice without the slightest hint of emotion. "I wanted to kill them, and erase their entire existence from the face of the planet… And I could have. No one would have ever known," she added, looking into Liam's eyes for a hint of his tacit approval.

"You would have known," said Liam. "And it might have felt good for a moment. It might have felt very good; indeed, but that is not you, Patrice." Hugging her tightly, he added "You have a beauty that many men covet, but only I will ever know. You scare them because you're all they've ever dreamt of, and more than they'll ever have in their pitiful, pitiful little lives. They bully you because they don't know what else to do with that cold hard reality."

While in Liam's embrace, Patrice felt invincible, and soon the dagger like comments of the detective seemed lightyears beneath them. She could hear Liam's strong level heartbeat as her head rested against his chest, and the soothing effect was like being submerged in a warm bath. She felt him easily lifting her into his arms and carrying her across the family room into the master chamber on the opposite side of the house.

Sitting her on the edge of the bed, he undressed her and laid her back on the mountain of pillows. Afterwards, he undressed himself before lying down next to her.

"One thing *is* true," said Liam, looking into Patrice's curious eyes. "My hands will definitely be full, banging my witch."

Deep into the night... They were.

CHAPTER 10

It was nothing new for locals to level unsubstantiated allegations and all kinds of veiled threats and insults at the residents of the Lafleur estate. Every guardian of the portal had endured these attempts at character assassination in some form or another during their long family history. From hooded pitchfork-bearing farmers to hypocritical pastors who showed up with their church choirs to sing at the gates, the house had hosted countless mock protests staged by people the guardians had helped on more than one occasion. While this was the first such attack directly leveled at Patrice as an adult, even *she* had experienced them as a child.

She and Naomi had spent countless breakfasts discussing the contradictory nature of human behavior. To Patrice, it seemed they preferred to suffer rather than seek the help Naomi provided free of charge the vast majority of the time. The only thing she ever charged for, were the Tarot readings mostly requested by the wealthiest families in the region, who for vanity's sake, wished to stay ahead of the rest of Shreveport's high society.

Others would bring relics discovered in attics, basements, and storage rooms out of fear that they posed a danger to their family members. Most of the time they were either harmless or their energies had been misunderstood by those in possession of them. As a result, the sheer number of these relics that found their way through the gates of the Lafleur estate was staggering. Patrice recalled how Naomi had simply accepted them, passing her blessings and thanks on to whoever might have dropped them off. Not once, did she ever admonish or wish ill will upon them.

"We are stronger than they are," Naomi would always say. "Therefore, it's up to us to look out for and protect them when they cannot protect themselves—including those who don't appreciate, or even hate us for it."

The reactions of the two detectives the day before was predictable if unexpected. People tend to demonize what they don't understand and based on the evidence they had to go on, it shouldn't have come as a surprise that they weren't there to make friends. Perhaps they were even trying to provoke a response that would reveal something helpful in conducting their investigation. In any case, they were fortunate that Liam was there to diffuse Patrice's anger.

Their unwarranted insults and accusations had nearly triggered a carnival of horrors because Patrice could have literally drawn and quartered them in ultra-slow motion just to make their suffering last longer before killing them. Inside the gates of the Lafleur estate, Patrice's power was already immense and still growing in intensity. Even though Liam could temper her actions to some degree, should anyone succeed in pushing her beyond her breaking point, heaven help them because there would be hell to pay.

In the meantime, Patrice and Liam had been working diligently to isolate and identify the source of the malevolent energy building along the outskirts of Shreveport, apparently to the complete unawareness of the local population. On the other hand, Nadine could feel the toxic buildup of spiritual evil growing nearly as fast as Patrice's power. The power emanating from the portal was also growing, as if preparing itself to receive something of monumental proportions. The energy field surrounding the house now extended all the way out to the gate which meant Nadine could survey the entire property and perceive the presence of everything inside it.

The portal was the power source, the house was the converter, Nadine was the conductor and

Patrice was the outlet for all of the energy produced. Liam only hoped he could figure out where to target all of that energy when the time was right, but he was never going to find it from within the confines of the estate.

"We need to look at everything from an elevated perspective," said Liam to Patrice. "We need to find the enemy camp—so to speak—so that we see where the malevolent energy is originating."

"I have an idea," said Patrice. "I'm not sure how well it will work, or if it will work at all, but what if we could scan the entire region all at once?"

"That would be Ideal," said Liam. "What did you have in mind?"

"I had a roommate in UCLA who was studying meteorology and she showed me a trick that might work for us," said Patrice. "They had a password protected website that could allow them access to a variety of weather satellites. They could scan for different atmospheric conditions by using a variety of filters to customize their search parameters."

Picking up her laptop, she walked over to the table in the study where Liam was sitting. "They change the password every year, but it was simple so the students could remember it. I think it was the word METEOR, and the current calendar year.

Of course, they were behind a couple of years, so I'm not sure anymore, but it's worth a shot."

Patrice quickly located the website and entered the password METEOR2017. It was rejected, so she tried METEOR2018 which was also rejected. The login portal indicated the next incorrect password would block the IP address permanently.

"Go with 2020," said Liam. "Maybe they were thinking ahead for this semester."

Nodding, Patrice said "METEOR2020 it is."

After entering the password, the screen went totally dark before lighting up again to display, WELCOME TO THE UCLA METEOROLOGY LAB.

"We're in!" said Patrice, excitedly. "Now, let's see what we can poke our noses into."

They quickly located the satellite imagery, as well as the historical data for Shreveport. Based on the nearly fifty-degree temperature difference between the outdoor and indoor temperatures at the estate when Patrice arrived, the search for cool pockets in the area seemed a logical place to start. Not surprisingly, their guess revealed some interesting points of reference.

On the color-coded map, warmer temperatures were displayed in shades of red, yellow, and orange. Cooler temperatures were in varying shades of blue, and the coldest temperatures were depicted in black. With temperatures in the mid- to upper-90s, virtually the entire map was awash in red, yellow, and orange. On normal internet image searches, the field is far too wide for anything other than general information; however, with these images the field could be narrowed down to specific houses or shop locations, which is why access to the system was controlled.

After comparing the historical temperature data for Shreveport, there was one location which consistently appeared as a black dot in the rear of a property near Caddo Street, and with each successive pass of the satellite, the spot became progressively larger. The difference in the images following Patrice's arrival was startling to say the least, because what began as a tiny dot, now enveloped the entire property.

"So, we have a location," said Liam.

"Now, let's see what the address is," said Patrice, zooming in on the property with a standard street-view internet map. "It appears to be a novelty store," she added.

"What say we pay them a visit," said Liam after writing down the address and grabbing the keys to Patrice's SUV.

"You mean, we should just barge in on them?" asked Patrice. "Doesn't that seem a little heavy-handed?"

"It's a place of business," said Liam. "Their hours of operation are publicly posted, and I see no reason why I shouldn't stop in to look for souvenirs to take home to Scotland with me. Besides, they may not even be aware that they're sitting on top of a demonic corridor. We could be saving them."

"You're serious about this, aren't you?" said Patrice. "Just what do you plan to do if we get there and all hell breaks loose?" she asked.

"Leave," said Liam with a shrug. "But we should take some of the Black Tourmaline from upstairs with us. It's been used since ancient times for protection and it's considered by many to be the most powerful protective gemstone. Since it works on physical, emotional, mental, and spiritual levels it should offer some added protection for us, no matter what we uncover," he concluded.

Leaving Nadine to watch over the estate, Patrice and Liam made their way across town towards the address on Caddo Street. During the drive, Patrice was certain she saw at least a dozen pedestrians carrying paranormal hitchhikers that they were unaware of. Not all of them were malevolent; some were simply unable to leave loved ones after passing, not realizing the emotional damage they were doing to their unwilling hosts.

Watching these poor people, stooped over and their faces riddled with worry lines without them even knowing why, made Patrice realize why her aunt had been so eager to help them. Some of them worked for years without achieving success of any kind because their creative energy was being siphoned off by these unwanted spiritual passengers. Even though the drive to the little novelty shop only took a few minutes, they were minutes that were very revealing to Patrice, solidifying her resolve to help as many of them as possible—even if they sometimes mistreated her.

Liam parked across the street from the little store, away from the circle of dark energy surrounding it. Above the door was a hand-painted sign bearing the name DOLLS & MIRRORS Novelty Shop. While the name sounded harmless enough, Patrice could feel the intense vibrations produced by the negative energy which had all but swallowed the little boutique. Even Liam could feel the tingle of the black tourmaline gemstone in the amulet he wore around his neck beneath his shirt.

"This place feels cursed," said Patrice.

As they approached the store, the shopkeeper seemed to have spied them through the shop window. By the time they reached the entrance, Patrice felt nauseous despite the powerful gemstone she wore. On the other hand, Liam felt absolutely nothing.

Outside the shop when Liam opened the door for her, Patrice said, "This was a bad idea," and turned to leave. Immediately, she felt an unseen force latch onto her, physically dragging her inside the store. When Liam attempted to enter the shop behind her, he was repelled backwards, and the door slammed shut right in front of his face.

"Patrice!" screamed Liam, pounding on the glass door with absolutely no effect. Inside, he could see the shopkeeper's grimace as an invisible energy held Patrice suspended in mid-air. Whatever was holding her aloft, seemed to be tightening around her as she struggled to free herself.

Outside, Liam was frantically ramming his shoulder against the door throwing his entire bodyweight into it, yet barely causing it to even rattle. Suddenly, he noticed the gemstone around his neck vibrating wildly. Tugging it from beneath his shirt, he wrapped the chain around his fist with the gemstone facing outward. Taking a few steps backwards, he took a running start and lunged toward the door, smashing his fist and the black tourmaline stone into the glass. It shattered as he crashed through it sliding across the floor covered in a layer of tiny shards.

Patrice was still dangling in mid-air, but she was no longer struggling. Her head appeared to be hanging downward and Liam feared she was being crushed to death. He felt foolish for bringing her here, with the main source of her energy miles away, while the person crushing her was standing in the epicenter of his power.

"Patrice!" Liam screamed again, feeling himself being pressed into the floor as if pinned beneath the weight of a grand piano. His hands were bloody as he clawed at the floor in an attempt to reach her, but the ever-increasing weight crushing him into the floor eventually made it impossible for him to even move.

Suddenly, Patrice lifted her head and looked directly at Liam. "Cover your eyes," she said matter-of-factly, as her entire body began to glow. The light coming from within Patrice expanded quickly, and her entire body seemed to ignite into an enormous blinding flash. The energy wave she emitted shattered everything inside the store, sending dagger-like projectiles in every direction.

Even with his eyes closed, the light expulsion was so bright it was nearly blinding.

After a few seconds, Liam slowly opened his eyes. From his vantage point, he could see the shopkeeper on his knees with his hands covering his face and blood flowing down his cheeks, dripping onto the floor. His body was riddled with glass splinters from the decorative display cases and mirrors formerly adorning the shop's interior. Patrice was still hovering in mid-air, but the dark energy which had been crushing her was gone. Now, she floated inside a sphere of glowing bluish-white light—the same bluish-white light that covered Liam like an impenetrable protective dome.

Now, it was Patrice's turn.

Raising her right hand, she lifted the strange man from the floor, pinning him against the wall formerly covered in glass display shelves and occult merchandise. She easily forced his hands away from his face and to his sides before casually floating over to within inches of him. It was clear to her that there was nothing left of the man this demon had initially possessed. He'd been gone for months; possibly years.

"Who are you?" asked Patrice.

"I am one of many!" spat the vile creature in defiance. "You are nothing! Soon you will be pleading for a death that will not come for you before being turned to join our legion!"

"You tire me," said Patrice, like a cat who'd grown bored of a dying mouse. With her right hand, she gestured as if waving away an uninteresting offer at a designer dress boutique. The demonic entity disintegrated into a thick black mass of microscopic particles, floating aimlessly before vanishing into nothingness.

After lowering herself to the floor, Patrice rushed over to Liam who, despite the ordeal they'd just been through, was for the most part, uninjured.

"Are you alright Sweetheart?" she asked, brushing shards of glass from his clothing as he rose to his feet.

"I'm fine Darlin," he answered, looking around what was formerly an establishment filled with occult merchandise. Now, one would be hard-pressed to find a fragment of anything larger than a postage stamp in the entire place. "Are *you* alright Patrice?" he asked.

"I'm fine too, but let's get out of here," she said. "I disassembled the demon temporarily, but this is the seat of their power and the source of the growing malevolent energy we've been looking for.

At best, this will only be a temporary setback for them."

As they headed out the door, Liam couldn't help but notice that the shop windows had remained intact. Patrice had actually limited the damage from her paranormal blast to within the confines of that particular shop. There wasn't even a single sliver of glass on the walkway outside as they hurried to their SUV and made a beeline for home.

When they arrived back at the estate, Nadine was there to greet them the moment they entered the house. "I'm glad you two are back," she said. "There's something I think you'd like to see."

Patrice and Liam followed Nadine up the stairs to the second floor. There was bluish-white light coming from beneath the doors of both rooms housing the artifacts, and upon entering the first one, they discovered the Eye of Idris... was singing!

CHAPTER 11

"When did all of this start?" asked Liam.

"Twenty-seven minutes ago," Nadine replied.

"That was almost exactly the same time you started glowing, Patrice!" said Liam, astonished.

"It was strange," said Patrice. "When the demon grabbed me, I realized the more I struggled the tighter his grip became. It seemed to be feeding off of my anxiety, so I relaxed and concentrated on the portal and the house. In only a few seconds, I could feel the energy building inside of me and it increased so quickly, I had to release it!"

"I'll say!" said Liam. "I saw the bubble form around me and closed my eyes only a second before you flashed."

"What was going on here, Nadine?" asked Patrice, still somewhat perplexed.

"I felt an energy surge coursing through the entire house, so I came up the stairs to discover both rooms were glowing around the seams of the doors. When I entered this room, there was light arcing from nearly every artifact on the shelves, and the second I stepped into the room, all of the energy from both rooms coalesced and shot through me, directly into the Eye of Idris. The beam released by the Eye, flashed like a lightning bolt, and shot through the window and outside the house. The Eye has been glowing and ringing like a tuning fork since then, although it has gotten much quieter."

"You're telling me that all of that energy was released in a focused beam through this window," said Liam, looking outside through the glass.

"Yes," said Nadine. "It was as straight as an arrow."

"Patrice," said Liam. "Come take a look."

As Patrice and Liam peered out through the window, there were signs of scorching on the bark of the trees, clearly marking the path the beam had traveled. While it was impossible to see the final destination of the beam through the thicket of trees surrounding the house, it had undoubtedly been released in the direction of Caddo Street— Exactly where Patrice and Liam had been earlier.

"This is amazing," said Liam. "Apparently, you were able to establish a connection to the house while you were miles away from it!"

"The portal must have felt we were in danger and sent me the energy to protect and defend us." said Patrice.

"Not only that!" said Liam. "It marshalled all of the resources in the house and transferred that energy to you from miles away and at nearly the speed of light!"

"I felt it," said Patrice. "It's what removed the anxiety feeding the malevolent energy inside the shop. Once I relaxed, I could feel the surge coming at me like a tsunami. I absorbed what I could, but it was so intense I could barely contain it at all, even for a few seconds."

"Now I know the purpose behind the Staff of Osiris," said Nadine. "It's a targeting device that allowed Osiris directional control of the energy beam released from the Eye of Idris without him having to hold it directly in his hand. It was one of the few items here that wasn't arcing or discharging any form of energy. In fact, it remained completely neutral throughout the entire episode."

"Then perhaps we should reunite the Eye and the Staff so we can exercise a bit more control over those energy discharges," said Patrice. "Luckily, there was a window here. Otherwise, that beam could have taken out the entire wall."

"I totally agree," said Liam. "But we need to perform a couple of experiments once they're joined, so we know exactly how the targeting system works under real-world conditions."

"That sounds reasonable," said Patrice. "Right now, I need to take a nap though. That burst at the novelty shop not only released the energy the portal sent me; it nearly drained all of my own."

Patrice and Liam retired to the master bedroom chamber. Within a few seconds of her lying down, Patrice was sleeping soundly. Liam continued his research in the library inside their room. Had it not been for Patrice establishing that long-distance connection to the house and the portal, things could have ended tragically. He'd let his excitement at finding the source of the dark energy, override his practice of following a thorough and pragmatic approach; a mistake which could have gotten them both killed. It was also a mistake he didn't intend to repeat.

While the daring decision did reveal the true natures of the Eye of Idris and the Staff of Osiris, it was not a risk he would normally have taken. With the type of energies at play here, mistakes could prove quite costly, and if Patrice was capable of harnessing that amount of power from several miles away, Liam shuddered to think what she could achieve were the portal, the house, the artifacts, Nadine, the Eye of Idris, and the Staff of Osiris all working in sync with one another. He could easily imagine that the legends of an energy beam capable of reaching beyond our galaxy, were indeed true.

There was still one phenomenon they had yet to discuss. In all the excitement surrounding the energy blast, they had actually skipped over a detail Liam thought was incredibly important. Inside the shop, Patrice had levitated, and she'd done so with an ease that belies the level of energy such a feat requires.

Even though the appearance of levitation is a popular magician's illusion, there are always some forms of cables and pulleys involved, whether they are seen by the audience or not. Patrice's levitation was no magician's trick. It happened spontaneously, as if it were the most natural thing in the world for her. Added to that, the ease with which she was able to steer herself was remarkable and certainly warranted further investigation.

Patrice slept for nearly three hours but awakened surprisingly refreshed and energized. After a light supper, she and Liam sat out on the porch to watch the fireflies. They'd only been outside about half an hour when Nadine appeared in the doorway.

"We're about to have visitors," said Nadine.

Not long afterwards, headlights shone up towards the house through the wrought iron gate at the edge of the property. A few seconds later, the intercom near the front door was buzzing insistently. Patrice answered it, asking "Can I help you?"

"Miss Lafleur," came the male voice through the speaker. "I'm sorry to bother you at this hour, but I really need your help!" the man exclaimed. "I don't know where else to turn."

Without a second thought, Patrice said "I'll open the gate for you. Just drive up to the house."

"Thank you!" said the man as the gate opened for him. The car came quickly up the driveway, stopping with the passenger side door right next to the steps. Getting out of the vehicle, was Detective Tate.

Liam arose from his chair on the porch, walking over towards the steps. "I hope you brought a warrant Detective! Otherwise, you can piss off! We have nothing more to say to you!"

Gently, Patrice touched Liam's arm. When he looked into her eyes, he fell silent.

"Please," said the detective. "This is not an official visit, and it's not for me."

Opening the passenger side door, he revealed a woman sitting inside. Her hands, legs and ankles were bound, and she was also gagged. "This is my wife!" said Detective Tate, trying to catch his breath. "She collapsed earlier, and I rushed her to the hospital. When she came to, she seemed to have gone insane; thrashing about and screaming in a language I've never heard her speak before. The nurse at the ER, Charlene Timmons, told me I should bring her here. She said you could help."

After a long expectant pause, he said, "I know that we were out of line yesterday; way, way out of line, and I'm sorry I didn't speak up when my partner went off the rails. I know that I should have, and I was wrong, so hate me if you will, but please Miss Lafleur. Please help my wife."

"Liam," said Patrice. "Please help the detective carry his wife into the study."

The moment he'd opened the car door, Patrice recognized the thick, tar-like shroud coating the woman from head to toe, and the appalling stench accompanying it. Nadine had been able to strip the spirit haunting Charlene from her prior to them entering the house, but this was literally a demon, and unlike Rayland's spirit, it was incredibly powerful, resisting even Nadine's attempt at dislodging it.

Liam and Detective Tate laid the struggling woman on the floor in the center of the study.

"Step away from her," said Patrice. "The demon riding her is going to resist vehemently, and once it's dislodged, it will latch onto anyone it can."

Taking a stick of salted chalk from her desk, Patrice knelt on the hardwood floor and drew an unbroken circle around the struggling woman. An impossibly long, guttural scream erupted from the mouth of the demon overlaying her, as the woman's hips bowed upward with such force, only the back of her head and her heels were still touching the floor.

"God almighty!" exclaimed Detective Tate, not believing his eyes. "This can't be happening!"

Nadine gripped the head of the demon, translating verbatim, its unintelligible words by using the knowledge of the grimoire inside Patrice's sanctuary. It said: "Tell Detective Tate what I made his wife do while he was at work! I made a whore of her! Tell him how many men I allowed to take her today and how many filthy things I made her do! I have been defiling her for days on end, and he is too stupid to even notice! Her insides are a cesspool filled with the seed of a dozen whoremongers! Tell him how his own partner was one of those men, and not only once! Tell him you filthy witch! Tell him!"

The demon continued its profanity-laced rant, twisting and contorting the tortured woman's body into the most obscene and impossible positions while gurgling noises spilled forth from her mouth as if she were choking to death.

Patrice approached, signaling for Nadine to release her grip. When she did, Patrice latched onto the demonic mass from outside the circle of salt she'd drawn around the poor woman's body. It continued to struggle, moving in jerking motions that instantly positioned the woman's contorted body into a series of bizarre poses which were literally anatomically impossible. The sticky black liquid dripping from her mouth resembled cooked blood and smelled like putrid flesh, and her eyes rolled back into her head as blood flowed from her tear ducts. The portion of her eyes that should have been white, instead was as black as coal, and the entire time, those wicked black eyes remained fixed on Detective Tate.

Behind Patrice, Nadine's glowing aura began to expand and brighten. The house was feeding her an inconceivable amount of power, and when she placed her hand on Patrice's shoulder, it flowed into Patrice's own substantial well of energy. The entire room was glowing brightly as Patrice telekinetically lifted and dragged the woman slowly out of the circle, forcibly peeling the demon from her.

As soon as the woman's body cleared the circle, the demon went berserk, still trapped inside it. Once separated from its host, the demon was no longer invisible, and both Liam and Detective Tate stared wide-eyed in disbelief as it struggled, unable to escape the salted chalk circle.

"Liam, I need you to take the detective and his wife outside. The house must be void of all possible hosts," said Patrice.

The two men quickly lifted the woman from the floor and carried her out onto the porch. When they were safely outside, Patrice sealed the demon inside a powerful energy sphere, and erased half of the salted chalk circle so that she could remove it from her study. With the contained demon now outside the circle, Nadine latched onto the sphere to reinforce it, and she and Patrice moved it toward the stairs and up to the iron door at the end of the corridor on the second floor. Her well-rehearsed hand motion opened the massive door to reveal the portal, already active with the gateway open to receive the struggling demon. Holding the evil entity in front of the portal, Patrice removed the energy sphere. The demon was instantly reduced to pulverized black dust and sucked into the gaping maw of the gateway. Once the demon was consumed, the gateway closed, the portal vanished, and the energy in the house normalized immediately.

Leaving the room with Nadine, Patrice closed the massive iron door before heading back downstairs and onto the front porch. When they arrived, Mrs. Tate was already awakening from her hellish nightmare. Although she was in pain from the physical abuse inflicted by the demon, she was also delighted to finally be free of it.

After sealing their spiritual auras against further demonic attack, Patrice prayed with them asking for deliverance from the evil hounding them and a speedy recovery for Mrs. Tate.

Liam and Detective Tate helped the frail woman into the car, but before Liam could close the door, she beckoned Patrice to her. Leaning in close to Patrice's ear, Mrs. Tate whispered "I know everything it said, and everything you *didn't* say." Looking into Patrice's eyes, she managed a teary smile, saying "Thank you."

Patrice simply nodded, closing the car door, and joining Liam on the porch. Before getting into the car on the driver's side, Detective Tate said, "You've taught me a valuable lesson Miss Lafleur. You could've turned me away, and lord knows I wouldn't have blamed you; but you didn't, and I am grateful."

Nodding wordlessly once again, Patrice smiled as Detective Tate climbed into the vehicle with his wife and drove slowly down the lane. Beyond the gate, they turned left onto the main road and disappeared into the night.

"That was the most intense thing I have ever seen!" said Liam, looking at Patrice with his arm around her shoulder. "You are truly a magnificent woman."

Looking closer, he said "Sweetheart, your nose is bleeding!"

A second later, her eyes rolled back into her head and she crumbled into his arms.

CHAPTER 12

Patrice slept for two days. Following the banishment of the demon from Mrs. Tate, Nadine moved Patrice into the sanctuary. Although Liam's first intention was to take her to the Hospital, Nadine was able to reassure him it wouldn't be necessary. In the secluded space of her sanctuary, the grimoire's energy could heal anything, as long as she was still alive when she entered it, and Nadine would carefully monitor her condition the entire time.

While Patrice rested and recovered, Liam studied. It was obvious to him that Patrice had been challenging the limits of her abilities, even as they were increasing day by day. After separating the first demon from the taxi driver and drowning it in the river, she was weakened but recovered relatively quickly. However, facing two powerful demons in the same day within hours of each other had apparently exceeded even her substantial energy reserves.

During Patrice's recovery, she slept deeply without waking, and Liam worked intensely, almost entirely without sleeping. He pored through every page ever written or documented regarding the Eye of Idris and the Staff of Osiris. Surprisingly, even after thousands of years of studying Egyptian history, there was nearly nothing regarding either the Staff or the Eye. Suffering through two days of absolute frustration, he finally discovered a thread, thanks to one of his colleagues in Egypt. It wasn't much, but evidently a professor in Cairo claimed to have proof that both artifacts not only existed, but that there were detailed instructions of how they were used.

While no one had ever published photos of either object, there were a handful of accounts written by people who claimed to have seen them over the past four centuries. These written accounts were in the possession of Professor Sayeed Nagi, and when Liam offered to show him the physical artifacts via video-chat, he agreed to share the information on how, according to legend, they were meant to be used. Following his near nervous breakdown upon realizing Liam did indeed have the authentic objects in his possession, they spent nearly three hours extensively researching Professor Nagi's notes on them.

While the house had used the Eye of Idris to come to Patrice's aid across the miles separating them, actually it had been an emergency measure that probably would have killed a spiritually weaker individual. What completely astonished Liam was that the energy from the Eye was meant to destroy the object it targeted; not enhance it. It was meant to be wielded by the user to project enhanced energy at targets as far away as distant galaxies. While severely restricting the energy pulse it sent to Patrice, normally the target on the receiving end would have been obliterated down to the atomic level. It would have completely ceased to exist.

Had they taken the Eye of Idris mounted inside the Staff of Osiris with them to the origination point of the dark energy behind the shop, it would likely have enhanced Patrice's own energy to a point that would have completely obliterated it and sealed it away forever. According to legend, it was actually capable of creating an independent gateway similar to, if not greater than the one inside the estate. The mere fact that Patrice was able to take a direct blast from it and recycle the energy into a powerful burst of her own, was nearly inconceivable. Suddenly, it was clear to Liam why her energy reserves had been so severely depleted.

Inside Patrice's sanctuary, the grimoire was doing its work, repairing her body, and replenishing her energy while keeping her in a near comatose state. The exertion had caused a minor brain hemorrhage which, save for the healing powers of the portal and the grimoire, would almost certainly have been fatal.

At the end of the second day, Patrice awoke to find a smiling Nadine at her bedside. "Good evening Miss Patrice," said Nadine. "It's great to have you back."

"Back?" asked Patrice. "What happened? Where did I go?"

"You collapsed following the strain of battling two separate demons and receiving the energy pulse from the Eye of Idris," Nadine answered. "I brought you into your sanctuary and you've been sleeping for the past two days while the grimoire restored you to optimum health."

"And Liam?" queried Patrice.

"He's been working nearly non-stop for the entire time you were resting. He's made amazing progress in his research, and I'm sure he will be anxious to show you everything... *tomorrow morning,*" said Nadine. "What remains of tonight should be used to cleanse your body and spirit with a warm herbal bath, prayer, and meditation." Before leaving Patrice's sanctuary, she said "Your bath is already drawn, and I will bring you something to eat shortly."

While she wished for nothing more than to spend the night in Liam's arms, she knew Nadine's advice had been correct. Whether on the other side of the house, or the other side of the world, Liam would always be there for her, and she was certain he would want her to recover fully before leaving the healing atmosphere of the sanctuary.

After bathing, she sat down at the small table in her room where Nadine had placed her food. It was a hearty homemade soup containing a variety of organic vegetables served with warm freshly baked bread. Following her meal, she reviewed the grimoire to better understand what had happened in the wake of banishing the demon. As always, Nadine had been thorough in her ledger entry and Patrice was thankful for the continuity she ensured.

She began her prayer and meditation session with deep breathing exercises that quickly relieved the stress from her body and cleared her mind. Soon, her spirit was at ease and her body was completely unburdened. What seemed like only a few minutes of meditation, was in real-time nearly three hours. Bringing her prayers and meditation to an end, she slowly opened her eyes to find Nadine was once again inside the room with her.

"That's new," said Nadine with a smile.

Before she could ask Nadine what she meant, Patrice looked down and realized she was seated in the lotus position while floating nearly three feet above her meditation mat! With a thought, she gently descended and came to rest. Rolling over onto her stomach, she extended her arms pushing up her torso and letting her head fall back while keeping her hips, legs and feet firmly planted on the floor. After two days of sleep, it felt great to stretch out her body, and despite the physical beating she'd taken, she actually felt amazing.

Upon completing a series of floor exercises, she rose to her feet stretching her hands toward the ceiling before finally relaxing and returning to bed. She could feel the house hugging her and seemed able to sense everything going on inside and around the entire estate. Even Liam was sleeping peacefully in their bed on the opposite side of the house. She wondered what he was thinking, and with no intention of intruding, Liam sensed her presence and welcomed her inside his mind to share his dreams with her.

The place they created for each other was a product of both their minds, without intruding into private spaces that should remain so. It was a place of love and belonging and absolute unity, and while separated by the walls and square footage inside the house, their hearts and souls were where they'd always been and would eternally belong: Together.

The next morning, Patrice felt admittedly better, and it was clear to all of them that her daily meditation time in the sanctuary was an essential part of being a portal guardian. In light of the mounting evil spewing from the ever-expanding dark energy zone near Caddo Street, the number of demonic possessions in the area was certain to increase. Without a proper daily recovery routine, Patrice's weakened condition could leave her vulnerable to a demonic possession herself; something the legion of evil would certainly welcome.

In the days that followed, there were multiple visitors to the estate. The majority of them were either simple hauntings or over-reactive individuals who'd convinced themselves they were experiencing the presence of attachment entities. Simple hauntings were usually resolved by either convincing the entity that they'd passed and needed to move on to the next phase of their existence, or by conveying an important message to the haunted individual from the spirit attached to them.

One spirit, while aware that she had passed, haunted her neighbor relentlessly. The man hadn't been able to sleep for nearly a week when he showed up at the estate. The spirit attached to him was that of a woman who lived only three houses down the street from him. She'd slipped and fallen down the stairs leading to the laundry room in the basement of her house. She had purposely closed the door behind her to prevent her yorkie, Daisy, from following her down the steps and now, the little dog was trapped inside the house, hungry and dehydrated. Once Patrice informed him of what happened and why the spirit was so desperately reaching out to him, the man rushed to the house to find the little dog curled up near the door leading down into the basement. He notified the authorities who discovered the woman lying at the bottom of the stairs with a broken neck.

The man took Daisy to the animal clinic where they treated her for dehydration and fed her. After only a couple of hours, the little yorkie was doing well, and the man didn't have the heart to leave her there alone. He took her home with him, where they both slept peacefully through the night, and the haunting ended immediately. The next day, he and Daisy came by the house to thank Patrice personally, offering her an envelope containing money. Patrice asked him to instead, donate the money to a local animal shelter, which he did.

Demonic possessions are completely different in that those malevolent entities were never human and seek only to inhabit a human host that they can completely take over and consume. Since the demons themselves do not require food or water, an extended possession will eventually kill the person they possess, forcing it to move on to another unwilling host. Such attachments must be dealt with as quickly as possible to avoid irreparable damage to the possessed individual. Broken bones and other injuries incurred by the host as a result of demonic possessions do not disappear instantly upon separating the demon from them. More often than not, the host will require immediate medical attention and time to physically recover from their injuries. On the other hand, the emotional trauma they suffer can leave deep and lasting scars that may never completely heal.

While hauntings are quite common, not everyone can sense the presence of the spirits attached to them. Demonic possessions on the other hand, are usually quite rare, and the marked increase in them was certainly cause for alarm, even among the local clergy. While Patrice was not the only person in Shreveport dealing with this surge in malevolent entities and demonic activity, she *was* the only one capable of dealing with the black well from which they were emerging.

With her spiritual energy now fully replenished and her connection to the portal's expanded realm of protection more solid than ever, it was time for her to return to the evil entryway and seal it off permanently. Liam's research had shed new light on how to effectively use the Eye of Idris and the Staff of Osiris and armed with this new information and Patrice's enhanced spiritual energy, the time to confront the demonic presence was upon them.

CHAPTER 13

With the investigation of the UBER driver's fatal traffic accident pointing in every direction *but* the Lafleur estate, Detectives Broussard and Tate were running down the list of other fares the driver had taken the night of the crash. The first two were airport trips; one delivery and one pickup. The third was a pickup from a shop over on Caddo Street to a gas station near Fatty Arbuckle's where Miss Lafleur and Professor McKenna had gone for dinner and drinks.

After reviewing the footage of the driver peeling out of the parking lot and driving directly into the oncoming cement truck, it seemed odd that his previous fare immediately hailed a cab… The same cab later discovered blocking traffic outside the Irish Pub. Having found no connection between Patrice and Liam, and the UBER driver's accident, they decided to pay a visit to the little shop on Caddo Street.

It was odd when they arrived and entered the store. Everything seemed staged, as if created for their amusement. Nothing inside the store had a price tag affixed to it, and the entire inventory seemed oddly… fake. After walking around inside the store for a few minutes, they were surprised to find a salesclerk standing behind the cash register they passed on the way inside the store. He seemed to have materialized out of nowhere because he had certainly not been there when they entered, and oddly enough, there didn't seem to be a storeroom in the establishment; nothing they could see anyway. When they approached the man, he seemed to be fixated on Detective Broussard, staring at him without blinking or even slightly acknowledging Detective Tate.

"I'm Detective Broussard and this is Detective Tate," he said, showing his badge to the salesclerk. "We're investigating a fatal motor vehicle accident that may be connected to someone who was picked up here only a few minutes prior to the incident. Do you mind if we ask you a few questions?"

A smile crossed the man's lips, but the look in his eyes seemed completely disconnected from the smile. It reminded Detective Broussard of the look a hostage would have on his face when his captor was hiding behind the door with a gun pointed at his head. Still looking at Detective Broussard, the man raised his hand and pointed a finger at Detective Tate saying, "He is protected. You are not."

"What?" said Detective Broussard. "Protected by who?"

"The witch," answered the man. "He and his wife carry her seal of protection."

"What the hell are you talking about?" asked the detective, irritated?

"His wife," said the man. "The woman you laid with while she was possessed. Surely you remember her."

Suddenly, Detective Tate was highly interested, asking "What the hell is he talking about, Frank?"

"The guy is nuts," said Detective Broussard. "Look at him. He's obviously strung out on something. You can't believe a word he says."

"You lay with the wife of your partner, and *I* am the liar?" said the man. "She was but a vessel of the legion, but you, Detective Frank Broussard, you laid with her because you wanted to. You have coveted her for months, spilling your sinful seed into her while she could not object, and you did so repeatedly before the witch..."

The man abruptly stopped talking as the back of his head burst open, spattering the wall behind him with brain matter as he slid down to the floor and vanished behind the counter. In front of him stood Detective Broussard. His service weapon was still smoking when he turned to face Detective Tate, who's weapon was already leveled at him.

"Drop the weapon, Frank!" yelled Detective Tate.

"You saw him Will. He was insane. He was talking crazy, trying to turn us against each other!"

"You just shot an unarmed man, Frank!" shouted Detective Tate. "Now drop the damn weapon!"

"We can fix this Will," said Detective Broussard, finally laying is weapon on the floor. "I have a drop gun in the car. As long as we stick together, we can..."

"There is no 'we', Frank!" screamed Detective Tate. "You raped my wife and blew an unarmed man's brains out. There is no fixing this shit!"

"She came onto me!" shouted Detective Broussard. "She wanted it!"

"So, it's true!" said Detective Tate. "You had sex with a mentally ill woman who couldn't consent. That is rape, Frank! Now turn around and get down on your knees and put your hands behind your head!"

"What do you want, Will?" pleaded Detective Broussard. "Do you want money? I can give you money. Just let me clean up this shit and get the hell out of here and I will give you fifty large tonight!"

"I did the wrong thing once, covering for your ass," said Detective Tate. "I won't do it again."

"It's that fucking witch, isn't it?" said Frank. "She got to you, too!"

"Nobody got to me Frank! You raped my wife and I just witnessed you murdering an unarmed man!" said Detective Tate. "You're as dirty as they get, and I'm going to make sure you go down, Frank."

"Then you're just going to have to shoot me, Will," said Detective Broussard. "I'm not going to jail over some junky store clerk and your whore wife!"

Suddenly, Detective Tate's eyes grew wide in horror as the man behind the counter slowly rose from the floor. His head was tilted at a curious angle and the bullet hole between his eyes was small compared to the huge one in the back of his head through which his brain material was literally dripping onto the floor behind him. In an instant, Detective Broussard's arms were snatched violently behind him and his feet scraped over a floor littered with the debris left by Patrice days earlier, as the mutilated monster turned his body to face it.

The illusion created by the dark energy enveloping the store vanished, revealing what looked like the scene of an explosion in an area that only seconds earlier seem like a completely stocked boutique. Detective Tate was frozen to the spot as the remains of the man behind the counter drew his partner toward it. After witnessing the demon exorcised from his wife by Patrice, he was far beyond disbelief but still found himself unable to move or look away.

"Did you really believe you could sleep with a whore of the legion without consequences, Frank?" asked the disfigured aberration. "The demon growing inside your bloated gut belongs to us, and it is time for you to bring forth our spawn."

"I... I'm not female!" shouted Detective Broussard. "I can't be pregnant!"

"Your rules of creation are of no concern to us," growled the ghastly remnant of a human being. "Bring forth our spawn... Now!"

Detective Broussard's belly began to swell as if it were filled with baker's yeast. As the skin drew tighter around his abdomen, his cheap blazer and shirt ripped open an instant before his stomach and intestines exploded, and a demon the size of a twelve-year-old child climbed out of his abdomen. The detective screamed in horror as he watched the demon spawn emerge from his belly, then turn to look him directly in the eye before it began eating his intestines.

An instant later, Detective Tate was physically ejected from the shop through the plate glass window at the front of the store. When he regained his senses, he looked back into the shop just as the demon's mouth opened wide enough to consume what remained of his former partner. Before his head disappeared entirely into the demon's bottomless gullet, he caught a glimpse of Detective Broussard's eyes looking out the broken storefront window at him. He was still alive!

Detective Tate scrambled to his feet and stumbled toward the unmarked police vehicle parked in front of the store. After vomiting out the contents of his stomach into the gutter, he climbed into the vehicle and sped away from the curb and down the street toward the Shreveport police station. When he arrived, Detective Tate parked in the lot behind the precinct and just sat there in the car. How was he ever going to explain this without being pulled from duty? Even he couldn't wrap his head around what just happened at that store. While he had witnessed Patrice separating the demon from his wife, he had still been a bit skeptical about the whole "sealing of their aura's" mumbo-jumbo. Now he realized that Miss Lafleur had probably saved him from a fate similar to the one meted out to his partner in that unholy horror boutique.

Patrice and Liam were in the study when she felt it. Something had entered our world and created a wave of malevolent energy so large, it seemed to have crashed into the protective barrier around the Lafleur estate! The demonic legion's champion had emerged and would soon be powerful enough to venture out beyond the confines of the dark energy sphere. Left unchecked, it would spread its evil roots deep into the surrounding suburbs, growing stronger with each subsequent advance.

While Patrice and Liam were far from experts regarding the Staff of Osiris and the Eye of Idris, they realized that sooner or later, they would have to actually use the artifacts to determine exactly what their effects would be. Up to now, they'd been careful to follow every possible protocol to prevent them from either injuring themselves or setting something in motion that they didn't completely understand. Having gone as far as they could go in their scientific investigations and theories, it was obvious to them that now was the time to put what they'd learned to the test.

Upstairs, they retrieved both the Staff and the Eye, and went out onto the second-floor balcony surrounding the building. "It's time to put our money where our mouths are," said Patrice taking the Eye from Liam and inserting it into the hook of the Staff. At first, she didn't feel anything and began to wonder if all the instructions had been interpreted properly. However, after firmly gripping and holding the assembled artifacts, Patrice felt her own energy flowing into the staff and the eye began to glow increasingly brighter with each heartbeat.

Liam watched carefully but did not speak in order to afford Patrice the absolute highest possible level of concentration. Even though there was probably nothing he could do if this experiment went sideways, he wanted to at least be able to attempt an intervention if necessary.

Patrice felt as if her energy and the Staff were one, transferring some type of charge up the staff and into the Eye. In order to better concentrate, she closed her own eyes while concentrating on the one mounted inside the staff. Her jaw dropped open in astonishment and she began shaking her head, saying, "Oh... My... God!"

"What's happening?" asked Liam impatiently!

"I can see," said Patrice with an ever-growing smile crossing her lips.

"You can see?" asked Liam, curiously.

"Yes," said Patrice. "I can see!"

He could see the staff turning in her hands, twisting back and forth as she gripped it firmly without preventing it from moving. Still a bit confused, Liam asked, "What can you see?"

After a long pause, Patrice said… "Everything. I can see *everything*!"

CHAPTER 14

"When you say *'everything'*," asked Liam, "Do you mean…"

"I mean everything!" said Patrice. "I can see everything, everywhere, at all times, no matter how big or how small; how near or how far. I can see the individual droplets of water in the fog bank off the coast of Puget Sound. I can see a single ant in an ant colony that has never even lived above ground, and I can see the individual hairs on that ant's right hind leg. I can see every star and every planet in every galaxy in every universe, even those whose light has not even reached the earth yet. I can count each speck of dust on a single asteroid in the asteroid belt. With a mere thought, I can switch from the planet Jupiter in our solar system, to the planet Corsicus in the Polymethanos galaxy, and every atom of every creature living on that planet! I can see every part of everything that exists here or anywhere else. I can touch the untouchable, hear that which makes no sound, smell the pollen on a flower that grows atop the peak of a mountain twenty billion light years beyond the edge of our galaxy, and I can water it with liquid from a stream in a dimension on the other side of a black hole which has existed for a billion trillion centuries, with merely a thought."

Upon opening her eyes, Patrice was immediately whisked back to the here and now, standing across from Liam who was completely mesmerized by the visions she'd been describing. In all of his research during the past several days and for the entirety of his career as an archeologist, Liam had never even imagined an artifact that possessed such power. The most amazing thing of all was that Patrice was the only power source energizing the Eye of Idris. The remaining artifacts in the house had been inactive the entire time. Her connection to the house, and thereby the portal, provided all the energy she needed to see through the Eye. Evidently, Nadine had been correct about the Staff of Osiris. It turned to locate and zero in on whatever crossed Patrice's mind in a nanosecond, and while it was glowing brightly, it didn't seem to generate any significant levels of heat the entire time.

"That was fantastic!" Patrice exclaimed. "There is so much more than we could ever imagine or hope to learn, and the randomness of it all, is almost symmetrical in its chaos." Looking at Liam, she said "It is beyond beautiful, even beyond perfection! "

"Godly?" asked Liam, curiously.

"No," said Patrice. "Idris did not create the Eye, nor did he forge the Staff. Both were a gift from one who lives even beyond the range of either of them, and *He* is truly God."

"You're telling me that for all the Eye allowed you to see, and touch, and taste, and smell and hear, there is even more beyond what you've already explored?" asked Liam.

"Yes!" exclaimed Patrice. "There is so much more!"

"Back to the task at hand," said Liam. "Can we use it to kill whatever demon crawls out of that hell-pit?"

"It is not a weapon, nor can it be used as one, for it can never take a life; not even that of a demon," Patrice explained. "The omnipotent God who created these for Idris, and or Osiris, did not wish for anyone who walks among us to ever take a life… Any life. In all the quadrillions of stars and planets and galaxies from here to eternity, life is a gift of the true creator of all things, and it is not within the judgement of men, or angels, or demons, or demigods to take without great consideration of every other possible option first. That is a right he has reserved for only himself."

"Then how are we supposed the fight such a powerful demonic spirit without the aid of these artifacts?" asked Liam. "Are we supposed to just let evil devour us?"

"We rid ourselves of them the same way all guardians around the world have done since the beginning of time. We send them forth to be judged by the god of all creation," said Patrice. "That is something we *can* use the Eye and the Staff for. We open a portal near the demon warrior and force it inside, where it will face judgement for its actions from the only one with the power and authority to do so. With the combined power of the Eye and the Staff, even a demon as powerful as the one brewing inside that black veil of evil, can be forced to face judgement for its actions," Patrice added.

"A weapon that isn't a weapon," said Liam. "What a novel idea."

"Which is exactly why it has remained hidden for thousands of years," said Patrice. "Mankind, in our perceived infinite wisdom, cannot progress with the knowledge of such an artifact's existence. Eventually, someone will find a way to corrupt its purpose and bend its benevolent energy to the will of an evil being. That's why there is nearly no written record of either the Eye of Idris or the Staff of Osiris. What of it that does exist, will appear when it is needed, just as my aunt Naomi always said. That is especially true for these two artifacts. The last time mankind faced this magnitude of evil, Osiris opened the portal and banished it into the nether realm to face judgement. Afterwards, he removed the Eye and buried it where it would remain hidden for over five thousand years."

"And when the evil reappeared, so did the Eye and the Staff," said Liam.

"Exactly," said Patrice. "Just holding the two assembled artifacts has shown me more of their history than a lifetime of study would have."

"Based on the rate at which the sphere of evil is expanding, that information comes none too soon!" exclaimed Liam. "According to Professor Sayeed Nagi, the banishment must occur on the night of the new moon. That is when the demon reaches both its full dimensions and its maximum vulnerability. On that night, it will use the cover of the moonless sky to expand and destroy everything in its path, creating a bounty of fresh victims for its legion of hell-spawned demons to inhabit upon rising from the abyss!"

"Yes," said Patrice. "That is accurate, which means we have only five days before that confrontation, and in anticipation of its arrival, the activity of malevolent spirits and demonic entities is sure to increase.

That spike in malevolent activity was already being felt in the clergy, by soothsayers, shamans, witches and witch doctors, paranormal investigators, and students of the supernatural all over the region. The accounts of hauntings and possessions seemed to be doubling every two or three days, and a number of individuals from in and around Shreveport had gone missing without a clue. Children's parents were calling them in sick for school, and employee absences were up substantially in a city where jobs were scarce to come by. Crime was on the rise and a few career law enforcement officers simply stopped coming to work. Hundreds of people were displaying signs of anxiety and paranoia, and violent confrontations between people who'd been friends for decades were also on the rise. It was all quite perplexing, especially since people were still hesitant to call the incidents in public, what everyone knew and spoke about in hushed private circles, demonic possession.

The constant atmosphere of helplessness, fear, tension, paranoia, anxiety, depression, rage, and mistrust added fuel to an already raging inferno. Evil thrived on these ingredients, and in Shreveport there were plenty of them to go around. Using the Eye of Idris and the Staff of Osiris, Patrice was able to locate not one, but five additional emergence points with demonic entities amassing beyond them in preparation for the new moon. They were located at the five points extending outward and beyond the original dark sphere in the shape of a pentagram. They would all need to be sealed quickly at the precise midway point during the night of the new moon. In order to practice and hone her skills in using the Eye and the Staff, Patrice closed her eyes and located five asteroids drifting in the belt between Jupiter and Mars. After mentally targeting each of them, Patrice began drawing on the energies of the portal enhanced by the numerous protective artifacts on the second floor. After only a moment, the items began to react, sending visible current arcing between them. Once their energy peaked, Nadine consolidated it into a glowing ball of energy that completely engulfed her before releasing it into the Eye at the top of the Staff wielded flawlessly by Patrice. Within the space of a single second, the eye released five distinct bursts of light into the heavens. Almost instantaneously, the five targeted asteroids were vaporized and once again, the Eye of Idris was singing.

With only two days left before the new moon, Patrice, Liam, and Nadine felt they were as ready as they would ever be. Patrice retreated to her sanctuary where she would spend the next forty-eight hours cleansing her aura and replenishing her spiritual energy through meditation and prayer. Liam kept precise GPS coordinates on the location of the emergence points, and Nadine held the entire estate under seamlessly overlapping surveillance, reinforcing the energy at points were demons and malevolent spirits attempted in vain to breach the perimeter.

Twelve hours before the new moon, the paranormal activity across the entire region came to a halt as suddenly as it had begun. People that had been possessed by tenacious demons refusing to let go of them, were suddenly free to roam about without demons piggybacking on them. Crime went from completely out of control, to completely gone, and the entire city seemed to be experiencing a Kumbaya moment after having been encased in evil for so long. The desire to toast the change in spiritual energy blanketing their town was palpable, and like most Louisianans given an opportunity to celebrate, this one would be epic!

While city officials called upon their citizens to exercise caution and avoid being lulled into a false sense of security, for people who'd been unwillingly hosting demons for days on end, they were happy just to be able to breathe again without coughing up blackish phlegm from their lungs. It seemed everyone in town was throwing caution to the wind and enjoying this amazing sense of relief at long last. With the sound of music spontaneously filling the air from a dozen different street corners and pubs all across the city, and the smell of mouthwatering Louisiana barbecue enticing people out into the streets, the party continued long into the evening with no end in sight.

While many members of the clergy, as well as paranormal investigators, Tarot card readers, palmistry advisors, clairvoyants, and even Voodoo priests and priestesses sensed the impending wave of evil building to a crescendo, their voices were simply too quiet to be heard above the frenzied cacophony of festivities unfolding all around them.

As the exact time of the new moon drew nearer, spiritual leaders and advisors all retreated to places of solace and sanctuary, thinking it was better to be safe, than sorry. In fact, you would have been hard pressed to find anyone in the streets with even the faintest sense of what the new moon might bring, because anyone with even an iota of knowledge regarding activities of the occult, could sense the shroud of doom hanging over the city like the Sword of Damocles.

At the Lafleur estate, Patrice and Nadine were ready, and the energy being generated by the portal was more powerful than either of them could ever recall it having been before—even under Naomi's stewardship. Liam watched in fascination from behind Nadine as she channeled the power produced by the portal, the house, and the artifacts, storing it for an unimaginable burst of energy into the Eye of Idris. Ahead of her, Patrice held her arms out to the sides, gripping the Staff of Osiris firmly as she levitated into the air above and just behind the house.

At 12:14 a.m. the ground began to tremble, but due to the sheer number of events in full swing, it actually took several seconds before people began to notice it. When they did, what began as a night of joyous celebration quickly devolved into the equivalent of a stampede as people began running for their lives, unsure of what to do or even where to go to take shelter from what they assumed was an unusually intense earthquake. That fear further intensified as an area spanning nearly a mile across, suddenly caved in, leaving a gaping black hole where the strip mall housing the DOLLS & MIRRORS shop had previously stood. The fiery glow emanating from it could be seen from several miles away, and within minutes, news helicopters that had been taking aerial shots of the various spontaneous street parties were redirected to capture images of the area surrounding the newly formed glowing crater.

They were just coming onto the scene over the cave-in when the enormous demon began clawing its way out of it. The Eye of Idris was glowing as Nadine surrendered the assimilated energy into it, and the Staff of Osiris had a direct target lock on the location. However, in order to prevent the demon from escaping back into the glowing fracture, Patrice would need to wait until it had completely cleared the crater before opening the gateway that would suck him back out of our dimension. Otherwise, it could slip back into the abyss, and reappear from another location on the next new moon.

The titan-sized monstrosity was standing defiantly at the edge of the crater screaming into the black night sky when Patrice launched the first energy bolt to create a gateway directly beside the demon. It had been prematurely celebrating victory for only a few seconds before it completely vanished into the dark, inescapable chasm. In rapid succession, the Staff targeted the five other locations identified by Liam, shutting them down and sealing them only a second after they appeared, preventing even a single demon from emerging.

The amount of energy discharged by the Eye of Idris in opening and sealing the demonic gateways was far beyond the sum total of all weapons ever detonated on Planet Earth. Even though the duration of all six energy blasts combined was less than one second, that momentary diversion of power from the portal inside the house had been the true objective of the demonic legion. That moment of weakness was immediately seized upon by the legion's champion, waiting within striking distance of the portal gateway inside the house!

Patrice and Nadine both sensed the breach immediately; however, from their position outside on the balcony, they were unable to reach the portal in time to prevent the powerful demon from exiting the gateway into the ironclad room behind the massive door. While the ancient glyphs and salted-chalk symbols worked with the iron floor, walls, and ceiling to weaken and slow the demon, Patrice's energy was so severely drained, that even augmented by Nadine, it was all she could do to keep from blacking out. Patrice handed the Staff containing the Eye to Liam as he and Nadine helped her back into the house and toward the sealed entrance to the room housing the portal.

Demons are masters of deception, and by tricking Patrice into focusing her full energy and attention on the six decoys, she'd been deceived into lowering her guard on the grand prize, even if only for one second.

The demon reached the massive iron door on the inside of the room just as Patrice, Liam and Nadine reached the outside of it. The tug-of-war match that ensued between them was truly epic. Patrice, depleted from the powerful energy bursts emitted to seal the external gateways, was pitted against the legion's most powerful demon, weakened by the iron room and salted-chalk incantations created to drain its energy. As these two powerhouses locked horns on either side of the incredibly heavy door separating them, neither of them was certain to win the battle which loomed ahead.

Initially, the constant back and forth motion of the multi-ton door, opening ever so slightly before nearly closing again, seemed to indicate the struggle might go on for hours! However, after several minutes of superhuman exertion, Patrice had given all that was left inside her, and collapsed onto the floor. While the house and the portal were once again fully energized, Patrice was far too weak to harness and discharge the energy necessary to close and seal the door.

As Liam knelt beside Patrice, attending to, and trying to revive her, the door began creeping inward, opening ever so slowly.

"Come on Darlin," said Liam. "Hang in there just a little longer and we can beat this thing."

Patrice attempted a smile, obviously in great physical distress with tears in her eyes, saying "I'm... so sorry my love. I... thought... I could do it. He's just... too... strong for me. Please... forgive me... Liam. I was hoping... we would have... more time together."

Kneeling beside her on the floor, Liam held Patrice in his arms; his own tears rolling down his cheeks. "Oh, no no no Darlin," he said. "You just need to catch your breath for a little while, and then..."

Patrice's head fell back, and her eyes closed. She was now far beyond the reach of Liam's voice. When Liam looked up again, the door was clearing the inner doorjamb, and despite the glowing incantations lighting the rooms interior, the demon inside was now clearly overpowering them.

Looking about frantically, Liam's mind was racing as he searched for a way to stop the embodiment of evil about to be unleashed on the world. Picking up the Staff of Osiris, he stood and walked defiantly towards the door, now swinging fully open into the room. The demon inside was enormous, hunched over so its head wouldn't scrape against the ceiling as it moved toward the exit, almost oblivious to Liam's insignificant presence.

Holding up the staff, Liam looked at Nadine and said, "Light it up!"

"I can't do that Liam!" cried Nadine. "The energy burst will vaporize you!"

"But it's the only thing powerful enough to stop that monster!" Liam Shouted. "Someone has to stand in the gap, and Patrice needs you, to get her into her sanctuary." Smiling at Nadine, he said, "It's okay. Just tell Patrice when she wakes up, that she's the love of my life and somehow; either in this life or the next one, I *will* find my way back to her." With a final flash of the smile Patrice so dearly loved, he said "Now, light it up!"

As Liam dashed into the room, Nadine focused every watt of energy that she, the house, the portal, and the two rooms of glowing artifacts could generate, releasing it directly into the Eye of Idris just as he leapt towards the giant fiend. The blast of light that erupted from it simultaneously ripped the demon into shredded black ribbons of dust, while instantly dematerializing Liam into brilliant particles of luminescent white light. Within seconds, the atomized remnants of both the demon's and Liam's essences were sucked into the gateway, and the portal closed, leaving the empty room behind them.

Nadine watched from the hallway as the aura of the room brightened and the portal disappeared. As if of its own will, the massive iron door slowly closed, sealing tightly as Nadine rushed Patrice downstairs into her sanctuary, where the grimoire was already glowing in anticipation of receiving her. After gently placing Patrice on the bed inside her chamber, she stepped outside allowing the grimoire to do its work, and for the first time in her entire existence... Nadine cried.

CHAPTER 15

The morning after the attempted demonic uprising on the edge of their town, the citizens of Shreveport awakened in an emotional fog. The ratcheted-up tension and amplified hate were gradually replaced by the normal everyday run-of-the-mill tension and hate that had been there long before the siege.

There were, however, a few subtle differences that, if one looked closely, were indeed noticeable. A general air of politeness among family members and long-time friends, people holding doors for strangers and keeping elevators open for others dashing towards them, and drivers actually stopping *before* pedestrians entered crosswalks and patiently waiting until they'd reached the other side of the road before continuing on their way, were a few small but visible examples.

People were checking in on their elderly and homebound neighbors and offering to run errands for them and bring them a warm meal or two. Simple acts of kindness, while still not quite commonplace, were certainly on the rise, and even protracted feuds and misunderstandings were finding new ears for explanations and apologies that were long overdue.

At the Lafleur estate, Patrice slept, and Nadine diligently watched over her not risking even the slightest chance that she'd awaken alone and disoriented. It took nearly a week for the healing powers of the grimoire to repair the multitude of burst capillaries and hemorrhaging blood vessels throughout her body. She'd suffered an aneurism during her battle with the demon inside the house and was also severely dehydrated. The gentle care she received in her sanctuary couldn't have been more effectively administered, and the grimoire kept her in mental and spiritual stasis as it addressed her dehydration and repaired her physical injuries.

There was, however, nothing either the grimoire or Nadine could do to minimize the soul-wrenching pain Patrice felt upon learning of Liam's selfless act. She remained inside her sanctuary for several more days mourning him, unable to face a world of which Liam was no longer a part. Nadine cooked for her and made sure she actually ate her meals; however bland they may have tasted to Patrice. It was nearly two weeks before she emerged from her bedroom chamber, oblivious to the bright sunshine and otherwise beautiful day outside the house.

Everything around her reminded her of Liam and she missed his enchanting green eyes and charming smile. Despite the melancholy that accompanied her like a dark cloud, she was determined to continue her work in helping to free others from the invisible burdens they carried. Perhaps by helping them breathe again, she could find new oxygen for herself.

The house seemed to know when she was ready, and as if sending out a beacon to those in need, people began finding their way to her. She helped them all without passing judgement on them or betraying their confidences, and surprisingly to her, it seemed to help. Each disembodied spirit she assisted in moving on, also represented a small step forward for her, and each person who's burdens she lifted, also seemed to remove an ounce of weight from her own shoulders.

The faces that came in to sit across from her inside the study were many, but to her, they were all like shadows coming and going at random without leaving so much as a wisp or remnant of an impression on her. She helped them all with a smile before sending them on their way with a prayer and a blessing, then retired to her sanctuary to cleanse and renew her spirit.

It was early in the evening when Nadine sensed the approach of a familiar energy from long ago. Joining Patrice in the study, she said "You have a visitor." Seconds later, the intercom buzzed.

"May I help you," asked Patrice courteously.

"I believe you are the only one who can," replied the calm male voice on the other end.

"Well, come on up to the house and I will do my best to help you," Patrice replied.

As they watched through the study window, the man approached on foot and walked up the steps to the door. Opening it, Patrice welcomed her visitor saying, "Good evening, Thomas McGee. Please come in?"

At first, the man was visibly shocked. With an apprehensive look on his face, he said, "You... You remember me?"

"Of course," said Patrice. "You were very attentive when I returned that U-Haul trailer several weeks ago."

"But... I mean before that," said the man, unsure as to whether or not she remembered the incident that had cost him two fingers.

"He is neither haunted nor possessed," observed Nadine. "But his aura is heavy; almost sad, in fact."

"Yes Thomas," said Patrice with a disarming smile. "I remember you from school and how you used to tease me every day."

Thomas hung his head in shame. He'd been half-heartedly hoping she wouldn't recognize him after nearly thirty years, but also quite relieved that she did, so he wouldn't have to offer her a complete rundown of their history.

"Please," offered Patrice again. "Come inside."

Finding his voice again, Thomas said "Thank you Miss Lafleur," before entering the house and accompanying Patrice into her study.

Inside her office, it was evident that Thomas had different expectations regarding how the house and her study would look. "This is not at all what I was expecting," he said. "It looks so… normal," he finally managed to utter. "I was kind of expecting…"

"A cauldron and a broom?" Patrice interrupted with a friendly smile.

Thomas had to smile himself, realizing in hindsight, how silly he'd been. "Yeah, I guess so," he said.

"It's alright," said Patrice. "Nearly everyone suspects that to be the case the first time they visit," she added.

"I think that has probably been the root cause of my own problems for most of my life," said Thomas. "People tell me I'm supposed to be a certain way, and pretty soon I'm marching down the road they've pointed me towards."

"Sometimes you just have to say 'no' to people, even if it means disappointing them," said Patrice. "People deserve their own lives and their own happiness, Thomas." Looking directly at him, she said, "So do you."

"When I was a kid... When *we* were kids... my mother didn't want me to like you," said Thomas. "She told me all kinds of things and made up a bunch of stuff about your family. It wasn't until years later that I found out the truth. She and your mom were rivals when they were in school. They liked the same boys, both of them were cheerleaders, and they were in constant competition with each other. Even after all those years, my mom refused to let bygones be bygones, and continued perpetuating a childish rivalry using me as her proxy, and you as the stand-in for your mom. It took me years to crawl out from beneath her shadow, and by then, you were halfway across the country and I never got a chance to talk with you again."

"Well, sometimes things do come full circle," said Patrice. "As you can see, here we are."

"I've always liked that about you," Thomas said. "Even when you were trapped out here in the sticks, you always had a positivity about you that made me envious. I didn't dislike you or anything, but you seemed to be happy, even when me and other kids were picking on you all the time," said Thomas.

Patrice listened without interrupting as Thomas continued, saying "That time I asked you out and you turned me down in front of all those other guys; I was glad you didn't say yes. All they wanted was to humiliate you. Of course, I couldn't let on that I was glad about it, so all those silly pranks and the teasing and bullying were mainly a way for me to save face." Chuckling, he added "It really seems stupid now when I think about it."

"It's a lot of pressure being a teenager," said Patrice. "Always trying to fit in with a crowd who probably won't even matter to us a decade down the road. Of course, we don't know it at the time."

"That's so true," said Thomas. "Once I lost my fingers and couldn't play football anymore, they dropped me like a hot potato. A year later, I was the one getting picked on. After we graduated, I came by your house a couple of times because I wanted to personally apologize to you for all the pranks, I pulled on you. For years, I've felt like I just couldn't move on with my life until I'd properly apologized to you. I'm glad I finally made it, and I am so sorry for tormenting you all those years ago."

"I forgive you," said Patrice. "And I would also like to apologize to you. Even if it was just a prank, I shouldn't have reacted the way I did. Your offer was actually very sweet, but I wasn't used to boys noticing me and I'd never had anyone ask me out before. I handled it badly, and I'm sorry we never got the chance to properly talk things out. I'm sure we could have been buddies."

"No doubt about it," said Thomas with a smile. Standing up, he extended a hand to her saying, "Thank you Miss Lafleur."

Accepting and shaking his hand, she said "Patrice. Please, call me Patrice."

"Thank you, Patrice," said Thomas, adding "And if there's ever anything I can do for you, please don't hesitate to ask."

"Thank you, Thomas," answered Patrice with a smile. "I appreciate that."

As they walked towards the door, Nadine mentioned to Patrice, "There's something upstairs that might be helpful to him.

Pausing at the door, Patrice said, "I'd like to give you something. Would you mind waiting here for just a moment?"

"Not at all," said Thomas, waiting patiently as Patrice headed upstairs to the second floor. When she opened the door, he could see a faint bluish white glow inside the room before the door closed behind her. When she returned, she was carrying an amulet made of Black Tourmaline in a men's platinum setting dangling from a medium length platinum chain.

Placing it in Thomas' hand and pressing it into his palm with her own, Patrice said "May the blessings of the universe find a home inside your heart, and may fortune be your constant companion and follow you for the rest of your days." After speaking her blessing, she opened the clasp and placed it around Thomas' neck, telling him, "Now, go in peace my friend."

Thomas was smiling as he walked back down the steps. Before heading out the lane to the main road, he turned to look back at Patrice saying, "Thank you. Thank you for everything."

"His aura is clear now," said Nadine, suddenly appearing beside Patrice on the porch.

"Sometimes, the things haunting us aren't ghosts or demons, but rather our own self-doubts and insecurities," said Patrice. "Other times, it's just the unfulfilled desire to get something from the past off of your chest. Either way, it feels good to rid oneself of them and finally move on."

As Patrice and Nadine stood on the porch watching Thomas disappear down the lane, in the distance Sirius appeared just above the horizon after its predictable seventy-day absence. Being twenty-five times brighter than our sun, it is the brightest star in the heavens and can easily be seen during the dog days of summer, when it sets after the sun in the evenings and rises before the sun in the mornings. The ancient Egyptians recognized Sirius as the representation of the goddess Isis, known to them as the bringer of life.

As Patrice pondered the volume of knowledge she'd acquired after meeting Liam and joining his team, she turned and walked back inside the house. Taking one last look outside, she caught a final glimpse of Sirius just before it flickered out, following the sun as it sank beneath the horizon. Sadly, she spoke aloud to herself saying, "Isis, now I understand how you felt after losing your beloved

Osiris." With overwhelming grief, she added, "My beloved returned Osiris's staff and eye to him in the underworld. Could you please ask him to return my beloved to me?" It was all she could manage to utter before breaking into tears again for the thousandth time.

Closing the door, she leaned against the wall in the entryway slowly sinking to the marble floor where she curled herself into a fetal position and cried herself to sleep.

She had no idea how long she'd been there on the floor when Nadine gently woke her. "Miss Patrice," she said. "The portal is active, and I have no idea as to why."

Quickly composing herself, she followed Nadine up the stairs. There was no light emanating from the protective artifacts in the two storage rooms, so the activity inside the portal was obviously not malevolent. Standing in front of the iron door, she placed her hand against it. It was expectedly cool, but in no way was it abnormally cold. Stepping back behind the salted chalk barrier on the floor before the threshold of the room, she raised her hand while spreading her fingers and moving it toward the door. It opened easily allowing her a view inside the room filled with brightly glowing light. There in front of her, backlit by the light beaming outward from the portal, was a figure she would recognize even a thousand lifetimes from now. Rushing into the room, she leapt into the arms of the only man she'd ever loved, and Liam's arms wrapped themselves tightly around her as time seemed to stand still around them.

His voice was warm and beautiful, and she reveled in the smell of him as she pressed her face against his chest. She felt his manly calloused hands gently cradle her face as he leaned down and kissed her lips with a passion that felt as if he'd spent and eternity in the underworld starving for her.

After a kiss she wished would never end, their lips parted, and she stared up into the face she'd dreamt of since her last memories of him holding her in the hallway outside the room. His magnificent smile was like sunshine, warming her heart to the core, and above them, the eyes that were as green as emeralds were now bright icy blue!

"Your eyes," said Patrice, gently touching his eyelids with her fingertips.

"They were so scorched by the blast that even Isis couldn't salvage them," said Liam.

"I don't care," said Patrice. "They've brought you back to me, and I will happily see for both of us!" she added, pulling his lips to hers again.

"It's alright Darlin," said Liam, smiling again. "Osiris, was so grateful for the return of his staff, that he fashioned these for me from the Eye of Idris."

"They're not green anymore, but I am thankful to have them." noted Liam.

"Like the rest of you, they are still beautiful!" exclaimed Patrice, before asking "Can you see with them?"

"Yes Darlin. I *can* see," said Liam. As his beautiful blue eyes began to glow softly, he told her "In fact, I can see... **Everything**!"

The End.

RIANO D. MCFARLAND – Author Information

Riano McFarland is an American author and professional entertainer from Las Vegas, Nevada, with an international history.

Born in Germany in 1963, he is both the son of a Retired US Air Force Veteran and an Air Force Veteran himself. After spending 17 years in Europe and achieving notoriety as an international recording artist, he moved to Las Vegas, Nevada in 1999, where he quickly established himself as a successful entertainer. Having literally thousands of successful performances under his belt, *Riano* is a natural when it comes to dealing with and communicating his message to audiences. His sincere smile and easygoing nature quickly put acquaintances at ease with him, allowing him to connect with them on a much deeper personal level—something which contributes substantially to his emotionally riveting style of storytelling. Furthermore, having lived in or visited many of the areas described in his novels, he can connect the readers to those places using factual descriptions and impressions, having personally observed them.

Riano has been writing poetry, essays, short stories, tradeshow editorials, and talent information descriptions for over 40 years, collectively. His style stands apart from many authors in that, while his talent for weaving clues into the very fabric of his stories gives them depth and a sense of credulity, each of his novels are distinctly different from one another. Whether describing the relationship between a loyal dog and his loving owner in **ODIN**, following the development of an introverted boy-genius in **JAKE'S DRAGON**, chronicling the effects of extraterrestrial intelligence on the development and fate of all mankind in **THE ARTIFACT**, or describing the parallels between people and the objects they hold sacred in **I FIX BROKEN THINGS**,

Riano tactfully draws you into an inescapable web of emotional involvement with each additional chapter and each new character introduced. Added to that, his painstaking research when developing plots and storylines gives his novels substance which can hold up under even the staunchest of reader scrutiny.

Possessing an uncanny flair for building creative tension and suspense within a realistic plot, *Riano* pulls readers into the story as if they were, themselves, always intended to have a starring role in it. Furthermore, by skillfully blending historical fact with elements of fiction *Riano* makes the impossible appear plausible, while his intensely detailed descriptions bring characters and locations vividly into focus.

Although it's certain you'll love the destination to which he'll deliver you, you'll never guess the routes he'll take to get you there, so you may as well just dive in and enjoy the ride which is certain to keep you on the edge of your seat until the very last paragraph!

Made in the USA
San Bernardino, CA
21 May 2020